TROUBLE on the TRACKS

ALSO BY DONNA JO NAPOLI

For young children:

Albert
The Hero of Barletta

For middle-grade readers:

On Guard
The Bravest Thing
Jimmy, the Pickpocket of the Palace
When the Water Closes over My Head
Shark Shock
Soccer Shock
The Prince of the Pond

For older readers:

Song of the Magdalene
Zel
The Magic Circle

TROUBLE on the TRACKS

DONNA JO NAPOLI

Scholastic Press / New York

ACKNOWLEDGMENTS

Thanks go to my family first; then to the personnel on the Ghan in the summer of 1992; Ed Gaynor's class at the Swarthmore-Rutledge School in 1995–96; Alexander Addison; Tony Addison; Shannon Allen; Brenda Bowen; Adam Bridges; Wendy Cholbi; Cindi DiMarzo; Carolyn Fraser; Michael Gelman; Jane Heald; Mark Heald; Gillian Ingram; David McKay; Beverly Michaels; Geoffrey Michaels; Julia Michaels; Lucia Monfried; Ramneek Pooni; Thomas Pouncy; Susan Revell; Daphne Riley; David Sobel; Lauren Thompson; and, especially, Richard Tchen, who batted around plot ideas with me.

Library of Congress Cataloging-in-Publication Data

Napoli, Donna Jo, 1948 –
Trouble on the tracks / Donna Jo Napoli.
p. cm.
Summary: While traveling across the Australian outback on a train, thirteen-year-old Zach and his younger sister, Eve, uncover an endangered bird-smuggling ring and try to save two trains from a full-speed collision.
ISBN 0-590-13447-7
[1. Smuggling — Fiction. 2. Birds — Fiction. 3. Railroads — Fiction.
4. Australia — Fiction. 5. Adventure and adventurers — Fiction.] I. Title.
PZ7.N15Tr   1996
[Fic] — dc20   96-27934   CIP   AC

10 9 8 7 6 5 4 3 2 1

Printed in the United States of America

First printing, April 1997
The text type for this book was
set in 12 point Janson Text.
Map by Elena Furrow

For Nick and Eva, who
worked it out

Love,
Mamma

CONTENTS

AUSTRALIA

Indian
Ocean

South
Pacific
Ocean

Cairns

Great Barrier Reef

Tennant Creek

Simpson's
Gap

Alice Springs

Todd River

Finke River

Tarcoola

Port Augusta

PERTH

ADELAIDE

SYDNEY
CANBERRA

Indian
Ocean

MELBOURNE

Tasmania

┼┼┼┼┼┼   Path of THE LEGENDARY GHAN

★   Capital

TROUBLE on the TRACKS

CHAPTER 1

Big Bird

"Look! There he goes again, the ballerina man!" Eve pointed.

I swatted at her hand. "Don't do that, Evil," I said, using my nickname for her that she hated the most. But I looked where her finger had pointed. There really was a ballerina man. I'd thought she'd made him up. My sister has been known to see things no one else sees. But there he was. Pink wig, a pink leotard complete with a tutu like the one Eve wore at her ballet recital last spring, and tall black dress socks with ordinary walking shoes. In his hand was a wand. Pink. He was very tall and very skinny and his elbows stuck out like doorknobs. It was hard to tell because of the tutu and all, but I think his butt was big. He looked to the side in a shop window and I could see that his nose was long, slender, and pointed. In fact, he was like Big Bird in almost every way, except that he was pink. He turned the corner.

"Come on, Zach, run!" Eve ran ahead.

I caught up. But by the time we turned the corner, the ballerina man had disappeared.

"He's magic." Eve's hands flew around in front of her chest in excitement.

I looked around anxiously, even though no one here knew us. Back home, Eve was always embarrassing me. I guess most thirteen-year-old guys are embarrassed by their younger sisters, but for me it was worse than normal because Eve was worse than normal. "Don't wave your hands around like a baby. And he looks more like a clown than a magician, anyway. He's probably on his way to a birthday party."

"Do you really think they do that in Australia? Have clowns at birthday parties, like in America?"

I didn't have the foggiest idea. We'd only been in Australia for a couple of weeks and we were tourists. "Sure," I said. Anyway, one thing I was definitely sure of was that this guy was no dancing ballerina. His costume looked like he'd picked it up at a thrift store after Halloween. Plus, he just didn't have the body for a ballerina. Plus, he was a man; men dancers don't wear tutus.

"We could pop into the chemist's over there and ask if he knows where the ballerina man went." Eve started toward the drugstore.

"No!" I grabbed her by the forearm.

"You're hurting me." Eve squirmed free and rubbed at her arm.

"Don't say *pop* for *go* and don't say *chemist* for *drugstore* and stop trying to pretend you're Australian. Everyone can hear your American accent." I looked at her arm. It was slightly red and I felt a twinge of guilt. But she drove me crazy when she spoke phony like that. I liked the Australian way of talking. I liked being surrounded by it. But I liked it to come out of Australians' mouths, not out of Eve's mouth.

Eve stopped rubbing and let her arm drop. "You're just jealous 'cause Mom says I have a better ear for languages than you do."

"Mom never said that." I shook my head to emphasize the point. "She just said you have a good ear. She never said anything about mine."

"See?" Eve smiled at me in her stupid, silly way. Then she burst out laughing like a maniac. Anyone who passed would think she was crazy. Why was my sister always so obnoxiously happy?

"If you laugh too hard, your head will fall off."

At that Eve laughed even harder. Then she did her imitation of a laughing kookaburra. It sounded like a dozen gibbons at the zoo back home in Philadelphia. I was sick of Eve's birdcalls. In fact, I was totally sick of Australian birds. When we first arrived in the beach city of Cairns, we saw this stupid little black bird with a white belly that flew down in front of us and wagged his tail around like a lunatic. He looked like he had an infection of the inner ear and couldn't keep his balance. Eve dubbed him Waggy, and mimicked his whistling song. Then when Mom was in the bookstore with us, Eve asked the bookseller if he knew the name of the little black bird with the white eyebrows that wagged his tail and sounded like this. She did her imitation and wagged her butt around and she said she called him Waggy.

The bookseller acted as though Eve was some sort of genius or something. He said it was remarkable that she noticed the white eyebrows. He said her call was perfect. (I gagged when he said it.) He said she wagged just like the bird. (I had to work to keep from choking.) Then he said the dumb bird's name was Willie Wagtail.

That did it. Mom decided Eve was a born ornithologist and bought her a two-volume set called *The Birds of Australia.* I don't know why Mom did it. Eve is an animal maniac in general — her interest in birds up to that point had been no greater than her interest in frogs or pigs or anything else. But once Mom started the stupid ornithologist thing, Eve really went at it with a vengeance. She identified birds everywhere we went after that. And imitated their calls. The more she knew it pained me, the more she did it. Right now her kookaburra call was making me want to puke. But at least she'd given up on chasing the guy in the tutu.

An old man who had been sitting on a bench in front of an art shop stood up and looked at her. He was an Aborigine — what Mom's friends called an "Abo." He came over, his bare feet dusty and pale in the sunlight.

I tensed up. He probably thought Eve was an idiot city kid who didn't know the first thing about birds. She was. But I was her big brother and, unfortunately, I feared it would fall on me to defend her honor — which was really unfair, because I don't think Eve had any notion of honor. The man looked anxious. I swallowed hard.

The man waited till Eve stopped. "It is taboo to imitate the kookaburra," he said in a thick, mellow voice. "The world might plunge into darkness."

Eve stared at him. She didn't look frightened; she looked awestruck. But I felt all nervous inside. Mom was an anthropologist, so I knew enough to realize it was possible this man really believed my sister had put the world in jeopardy. And if he did, what would he do now?

The man rubbed his throat just under his scraggly beard, while I tried to decide what to do if he should suddenly attack her for breaking the taboo. On the one hand, she didn't know she was breaking a taboo. The man should know that. After all, we were clearly tourists, and all the people in Alice Springs were used to how dumb tourists were. On the other hand, Eve was the most annoying ten-year-old in the world. Maybe the man knew this instinctively and would decide to rid the world of her. It might not be such a bad decision. On the third hand, she was my sister.

I knew I could outrun this old guy, but I knew just as well that Eve couldn't. Plus, she still didn't seem to realize the danger — she might not run even if he attacked. She stood frozen like a statue right in front of him and looked up at his face as though he were some sort of a hero. I kept my arms by my sides, but my hands were ready. Physically, I'm not too big myself. But I wrestle and play baseball, and I fence. I didn't want to fight, but if I had to, I would.

The man stopped rubbing his throat. "Try this." He whistled a high, sweet melody. When he stopped, he touched Eve on the shoulder. "Try."

"Is it the butcherbird?" Eve's face was as sweet as the melody. I had the urge to punch her. I've

7

never punched Eve — though I've wanted to many times. But she had to be wrong now. How could a bird with a name like "the butcherbird" have such a lilting call? It would be good to hear this man laugh at her. Maybe even yell at her.

The man smiled. He repeated his birdcall.

I couldn't believe it. My sister had broken a taboo that was probably sacred to this man, and here he was forgiving her and smiling at her just seconds later. Was the whole world crazy? How could Eve charm everyone so easily?

When the man finally paused, Eve copied him.

The man joined her.

By this time, people on the sidewalks had stopped to listen. Many of them smiled. One woman wearing tan shorts and a bush hat dropped some coins by the birdcallers' feet.

I took Eve's hand and pulled her after me. "We've got to go home," I mumbled. I held her fingers tight so she'd know not to protest.

Eve walked backwards, waving, as I dragged her away. "I was having fun. Why'd we have to leave so soon?" So much for her getting the message not to protest.

I pressed my mouth closed and grimly led my ridiculous sister the two blocks home to our motel. The next to the last day of our stay in Alice Springs was ruined.

At four o'clock the next afternoon, I kissed Mom good-bye — one clean peck on the cheek, nothing sappy. I slipped Eve's backpack off my right shoulder and set it on the floor of the compartment. It was heavy — heavier than mine. Probably because of her dumb bird books. I was carrying it for her because she had run ahead onto the train and left it just sitting there on the train platform like the ninny she is, and Mom had looked at me with that "please" look of hers. I was doing it for Mom, not for Eve. After all, I was the man of the household and had been since I was six — since Dad died.

I pushed Eve's backpack into the corner with my foot. Then I slipped my own backpack off my left shoulder. I sat down on the cushioned train seat and tried to look calm. I was about to take a ride on the most famous train in all of Australia — "The Legendary Ghan." I'd read all about it in the brochure Mom picked up yesterday. Only two trains in the whole world have pianos on them, and the Ghan is one. Plus, it had an entertainment car for kids, complete with videos and an arcade. And our compartment came with a shower. I was going to actually take a shower on a train! Legendary indeed. I sat tall; the moment required a certain decorum. But Eve didn't seem to know that. She clung to Mom and kissed her repeatedly.

"It'll only be a few days," I said in exasperation.

Eve took no notice. She went on hugging Mom. What a bug she was. Worse than a bug, a worm. She's the one who had run ahead to get on the train and now she was hanging on Mom like the trip ahead was some terrible nightmare. And Mom stroked her hair as though Eve needed comfort.

"It's a great train," I said. There was a tourist magazine sitting right on our train seat, and across the front were the words "The Legendary Ghan." I picked it up and pointed. "See? It's a legend. What's the matter with you?"

All of the sudden Eve let go and sat down beside me. "Zach's right, Mom. You can go now."

She lifted her chin as if she was being supremely brave. "We'll be fine."

"Oh, my big children! You're so grown up." Mom smiled at us both, but I could see the worry in her eyes. "Zach, take care of her."

"Yeah," I said. "I'll keep an eye on it." I jerked my thumb at Eve.

Mom gave me one of her meaningful looks. "Please. Your sister isn't an 'it.' I know you love her — and she knows you love her — in spite of how you talk. But, still, you can talk more sweetly." She smiled coaxingly. I was about to relent when she said, "You can be kind to her for twenty-two hours, can't you?"

After a build-up like that, I had no choice: "Nope," I said.

"Oh, Zach! Eve's so young. And that's all the train trip will be — just twenty-two hours. And Aunt Kelly will be waiting for you when you get off the train in Adelaide."

Mom looked so worried by now that I felt sorry for her. "I was joking, Mom. I'll be nice. We'll have a good time."

Mom nodded and flitted her eyes around the compartment. "It should be very comfortable.

11

You've got your own toilet." She opened the bathroom door. "Did you see how to pull down the toilet seat, Eve? It folds out from the wall. And the sink, too. And . . ."

The train whistle blew.

I got up and gently ushered Mom out into the corridor. "We're going to be just fine, Mom. Don't worry about a thing. You have to get off before the train heads out or you'll wind up coming with us and missing your chance to do your fieldwork at the Aboriginal settlement."

Mom's eyes glowed for a moment. I had struck a chord. Mom was studying a community that spoke a language called Walpiri. There were only a few hundred people — and they had their very own language. It would have been as though my middle school back home had its own language that only the students spoke. Weird. Anyway, Mom loved the whole thing. She'd been talking about her work all week. She was looking forward to it. Her face was happy. Then she blinked and the worried look returned. "Some-times I get too overprotective," she muttered, half to herself. I'd heard her say that under her breath about a million times before. Once I'd listened while Mom told an old friend how hard it had been after Dad's death. How she'd wanted to lock us all up in the house and never let us go outside — into the danger of the world. But she didn't lock us up. She let us go everywhere and do everything. Except she worried the whole time we did it.

She rubbed her hands together now and went back into the compartment to give Eve a final kiss and hug. "Your carriage is just about in the center of the train. If you want to go to any of the public carriages, with the food or entertainment, walk that way, toward the end of the train." Mom pointed. "The other way is nothing but sleeper compartments." Mom kissed Eve again.

Then she came out into the corridor, took my hand, and pulled me behind her. Ours was the next to the last compartment of our carriage. But Mom didn't go to the closest exit — she went all the way down to the other end of the carriage. I knew she did it to stay with me as long as possible. I followed her to the end of the train carriage and stood in the doorway as she went down the steps.

She turned and kissed me again and finally let go of my hand. "I love you, Zachary. Try to be good to Eve. She loves you, too, you know."

"Yeah, sure. I won't feed her to the crocodiles." That was a dumb thing to say, because there weren't any crocodiles where we were going, but I couldn't think of anything else. I looked at the top of Mom's head and realized I'd probably grown that final inch that made me as tall as her. "You take care of yourself, too."

Mom smiled. "You're so sweet, Zach. To everyone but Eve."

I scratched my cheek and looked at the floor. "I'll be nice to her, Mom."

"I know you will." Mom fumbled with the cloth bag over her shoulder. "Do you think the twenty dollars I gave you is enough? I could give you more."

Money was always an issue. And she'd already put out enough for the train tickets. We were going first class, because that's the only way they would take us without an accompanying adult. A porter was supposed to check up on us regularly for that price, and we were supposed to get everything we needed. But, still, the cost was terrible. "We won't even spend the twenty," I said. "All our meals are included. Bye, Mom."

Mom stepped back from the train hesitantly. That's when I saw the tall, skinny Big Bird ballerina man talking to the conductor. He wasn't in his ballerina costume anymore, but it was him, all right. No one else had that nose and those elbows and, especially, that butt. His normal brown hair showed under one of those expensive bush hats called an Akubra, the kind I had wanted to buy. I tugged at the edge of my own cotton hat, a five-dollar special from the Disposal store (Australia's equivalent of an Army-Navy store). The tall man was holding a huge square box by a ring at the top. It had a black cloth draped over the whole thing. The conductor walked around the box, talking. Irritation showed clearly on the tall man's face. Then he seemed to think better of it. He actually smiled. The train whistle blew again. The tall man lifted one side of the black drape. From my position, I couldn't see what was under that drape, but the conductor could. He seemed satisfied finally, and the tall man climbed up the steps at the other end of the same train carriage that Eve and I were staying in. The conductor followed him in and shut the door. The door in front of me shut automatically. The train pulled out.

I waved to Mom through the glass of the top half of the door. But her eyes weren't on me; she was already waving to Eve, whose face I imagined pressed against the glass of our compartment window. Good-bye, Alice Springs, I thought. Good-bye, Mom. And I didn't feel the slightest bit of sadness. A separation for a few days would do us all good. And Mom could take care of herself. I didn't need to worry about her, even if she worried about us.

The train picked up speed quickly. I walked back down the corridor toward our compartment, debating whether to go give Eve a comforting big-brotherly smile or start out on the right foot and jump in on her, growling and clawing the air. I didn't get a chance to do either, though. Eve stood in the corridor talking to the tall man.

"Can't I see, even if they're not real?" Eve held her hands behind her back. That's what

Mom always told her to do when she was having trouble keeping her hands off things.

"You're a curious one, aren't you?" The man's voice was strained. For once I'd met someone who saw Eve for the menace she was. I liked this irritable ballerina man. But the man was moody and he changed moods right then — just as he'd finally smiled at the conductor and showed him what was under the black cloth, he now smiled at Eve and lifted a corner of the cloth. I leaned forward and looked, too.

"Fake crows?" Eve wrinkled her nose at the big, black, artificial birds. "Why on earth would you bring a huge birdcage with fake crows in it onto the Ghan?"

"They're part of our act," said the tall man.

"Oh!" Eve clapped her hands together. "So you are clowns, after all. My brother guessed that."

The man looked at me and raised an eyebrow. "You her brother?"

I didn't think he'd believe me if I denied it. I nodded.

"How'd you decide I was a clown?"

"We saw you," said Eve. "We saw you on the street in your tutu. I have one just like it." She bit her bottom lip. "But your socks didn't look so good with it."

"And you recognized me now, out of costume?" The man frowned.

"Oh, it was easy," said Eve. "You have a nose like an ibis beak."

"What?"

I took Eve by the arm. "We've got to go in our compartment now," I said. I pulled her after me and the man banged around behind us, finally managing to get the big birdcage into his compartment. Once I'd shut us inside our own compartment, I lit into her. "Why did you say that? You can't go telling people they have a nose like a bird beak."

Eve unzipped her backpack and pulled out volume one of her bird book. She flipped through the pages and then held the book out to me. "See."

I stared at the Straw-necked ibis. I recognized it — the seaside town of Cairns had been covered with this kind of bird. And Eve was right — the man's nose had the same curve as the ibis's beak. I had realized, of course, that his nose was beak-like. But it took Eve's eye to see it was an ibis beak. The fact that she was so observant made me angry. "That's not the point. It doesn't matter if it's true. It's insulting to say someone looks like a bird. You're ten years old. You know better."

Eve stared at me with big round eyes. "I was sure he'd understand, being a bird lover and all . . ." Her stupid happy face was sad for once.

I looked out the window. The countryside was already completely deserted. Deserted desert. No sign of Alice Springs. We were out in the middle of sand, miles and miles of red sand and low bushes in every direction. The anger left me as suddenly as it had come. "It's okay, Eve. Get out your book. We're going to read until the porter calls us to dinner."

"I don't want to read." But Eve obediently reached into her pack and pulled out *Watership Down*.

"How much have you read?" I asked, trying to sound interested. After all, she hadn't meant to insult Beak Man — she just didn't think. It wasn't her habit to think too much.

"Just the beginning."

"The beginning is the most boring part," I said. "But then it gets great."

"I think the beginning is the best part I've read." Eve opened the book.

"How can you say such a stupid thing?" I yelped. "The beginning is the only part you've read."

"Oh." Eve looked at me. She giggled. "Yeah."

I got out my own book and read.

After a while, Eve said, "Guess what we're having for chicken."

I looked at her.

"Ooops," she said. She giggled again. "I meant, 'Guess what we're having for dinner.'"

"Chicken," I said. I went back to my book.

"Yeah," whispered Eve. She moved closer to me and turned the page of her book. I glanced over and saw that she was only on page five. The book was too hard for her. That's what she got for always trying to keep up with me. She moved closer still. "Yeah. Chicken is good," she said. Then she laughed. "I bet it's a lot better than stuffed crow."

I didn't even bother to look at her. Some of the things she said were too stupid to deserve an answer. Twenty-two hours, and only about half of one was gone already. That meant twenty-one-and-a-half very long hours to go. I felt beat already.

CHAPTER 2

The Key

Someone rapped on our compartment door three times.

I looked up from my book. "Who is it?"

Eve got up and opened the door.

The man had on a white short-sleeve shirt, black pants, and a black bow tie. He smiled. "I'm your porter. My name's Eugene. How's everyone doing in here?"

I smiled back. "Fine."

Eve licked her lips. "When's dinner?"

"Oh, you're hungry, are you?" Eugene laughed. "That's exactly what I came to see you about. You have your choice of a five-thirty, six-thirty, or seven-thirty sitting."

"We'll take five-thirty," said Eve.

"That's fine. Just tell the conductor when he comes around and he'll give you tickets. But you better realize that a five-thirty dinner means you're in the seven-thirty breakfast group tomorrow morning."

"Yikes." During the school year I had to get up at six every day in order to make the seven o'clock bus. I looked forward to sleeping late in the summer. "What if we go at six-thirty?"

"Then breakfast will be at eight-thirty."

"We'll go at six-thirty."

"I'm hungry," said Eve.

"We'll go at six-thirty," I said firmly.

Eugene nodded. "And will you have tea or coffee before breakfast tomorrow?"

"Why?" said Eve.

"Why?" Eugene laughed again. Eve had obviously charmed him in two seconds flat. It didn't make sense — he didn't seem like a moron. "Because I'll bring you what you want. You get your warm drink here in your compartment. Then you can go off to the dining car for your breakfast."

Eve seemed to think about that. "I want milk."

"One milk," said Eugene. "That would be fine."

"I'll take tea," I said.

"One milk and one tea. And will you have milk and sugar in your tea?"

"Yes." I gave a quick nod. Then I added, quite smoothly, "That would be fine."

"I changed my mind," said Eve. "I'll have tea with milk and sugar, too. Lots of sugar."

"Very well," said Eugene. "Two teas." He smiled and left, shutting the door behind him.

Eve sat down beside me. "What do we do till dinner?"

"Read," I said. I opened my book and looked down at it.

"I'm sick of reading." Eve fidgeted around. "Let's sing."

"No."

"Take me out to the ball game," she sang, not getting the tune quite right. "Take me out to the fair. I don't care about the stupid game. All I want is the food!"

"Stop singing!"

"Well, it's true." Eve scratched her elbow. "The whole song is about peanuts and Cracker Jacks. She doesn't care at all about the boring game."

"Baseball isn't boring," I said.

"Well, excuse me, Mister Ballcatcher."

Eve had picked up that excuse-me line from her best friend back home. I hated it. "I don't play catcher. I'm an outfielder."

"Oh." She giggled.

"There's nothing funny about it. Why do you think everything's funny?"

"I don't know. Maybe everything is." She giggled again. "Don't you hate it when you have to pee and you have your pants on?"

I put down my book. "Evil, you can't ask questions like that."

"Well, it's very annoying." She got up and opened the bathroom door. She tugged at the toilet seat. She banged on it. She kicked it. I finally got up and pulled it down for her. "Thanks." She smiled at me. I backed out and shut the door.

I opened my closet (we each had one) and took out the extra pillow stuffed in there. On the inside of the door was a semicircular metal rod. I stared at it for a second before I realized it was a hat rack. Australians don't go anywhere without their hats. The thought made me happy. I like figuring out things like that. I fished my five-dollar hat out of my backpack and stuck it in the rack. Then I shut the closet and settled myself on the seat with the pillow at my back.

A moment later Eve came out of the bathroom.

"You forgot to flush," I said.

Eve wouldn't look at me. "I don't want to flush."

"Why not?"

"Who knows what will happen?" She sat down and picked up her book.

I had to admit it: sometimes Eve seemed like such a little kid, I almost felt sorry for her. I got up and flushed the toilet and pushed it back up against the wall again. "See, nothing happened."

"That time," said Eve. "How long till dinner?"

I looked at my watch. "Long."

"How long?"

"Long enough for me to read a chapter or two if you'll stop talking."

"Well, excuse me!" Eve sat down. Then she got up, opened her closet, took out her extra pillow, and came back and sat down. She fidgeted around. "Oh!" she said loudly in a happy voice. She unzipped her backpack, reached down under her clothes, and brought out a big greenish-yellow fruit, the size of a cantaloupe. So that's what had made her backpack so heavy: five pounds of fruit on top of five pounds of bird books. "Where's your knife?"

I got out my knife.

Eve extended her hand. "Well, give it to me."

"It's my knife."

Eve handed me the fruit. "Then you cut it."

I didn't know what was inside. Maybe all sorts of putrid stuff would come dribbling out. I put the fruit back on her lap and turned my knife over and over in my hands. Mom didn't like Eve using knives. She was ridiculously protective of Eve. I'd never understood that. Finally, I opened the knife and held it out. "It's a lockback. You can't hurt yourself. Here."

Eve took the knife and promptly stabbed the fruit. If the knife hadn't been a lockback, it would have closed on her fingers for sure. Maybe

Mom was right not to let Eve do anything dangerous. If I demanded the knife back, she'd probably refuse and get even more wild with it. I cringed inside while she carved at the fruit savagely till she had a ragged hunk in her hand. When she finally gave back my knife, I had to suppress the urge to sigh in relief.

We both looked inside the open fruit. The middle was filled with little black balls.

"Rabbit droppings," I said.

Eve giggled. The hunk in her hand was bright orange. She handed it to me. "Try it."

"What is it?"

"Paw paw."

"Never heard of it."

"Sure you have." She thrust forward her chin and sang, "Picking up paw paws, Put 'em in the basket, Way down yonder, In the paw paw patch."

"It's 'put 'em in your pocket,' not 'in the basket.'"

"Who's got a pocket big enough for this thing?"

"No more singing." I took a bite of paw paw.

Eve watched me. I handed back the paw paw and she took a bite.

We both sat back and looked out the window, chewing on the half-slimy flesh of the fruit. The ground outside was rust red. Every now and then it changed to pale orange sand, then back to red.

"Paw paw's not great," said Eve.

"No."

"Oh, well." She looked around. She got up and set the paw paw on the top of the tiny trash receptacle that stuck out of the wall. The paw paw rocked with the rhythm of the train. "I asked Mom if I could buy one, you know, just to have the experience." She sat back down. "It was worth a try."

"Sure." There was something sort of dejected about the way she gave up on the paw paw so fast. Against my will, I felt sorry for her again. "It's fun to try new things."

"Zach?"

"Yes?"

"How much would you weigh without your skin?"

I considered her face. She was serious. Why

these questions came to her I'd never understand. "How should I know?" I looked out the
window again.

"Zach?"

"What now?"

But right then a loud, harsh *"Kree, kree, kree,"*
came from the other side of the compartment
wall.

I jumped up in surprise.

Eve went to the door.

I got in front of her. "Where do you think
you're going?"

"To see the clown and his bird, of course."

"What?" I felt stupid and confused, and angry
that Eve didn't seem to feel either. "Have you
lost your mind?" I blustered. "The clown has
fake crows." I thought about how the conductor
had given the clown a hard time when he was
standing on the train platform with the covered
birdcage. "And they wouldn't allow real animals
on the Ghan, anyway. At least not anywhere but
in luggage, I'm sure."

Eve looked disappointed. "I know that —
about the animals, I mean. But it sure sounded
real." Then she gave a sudden smile. "So,

obviously, he's good at birdcalls. Terrific, in fact. That was a cockatoo scream."

"How could you know it was a cockatoo scream?"

"Nothing else sounds like a cockatoo. They're one of the easiest to identify."

I thought about that. She sounded right. "So what? That's no reason to go bother him."

"I won't bother him. I'll just ask him to make birdcalls for me." She smiled. "What can that hurt? Come on, Zach. Don't be a grump all the time."

"I'm not a grump all the time." The accusation stung. It wasn't true. I mean, okay, even I could see that Eve made me grumpy a lot. But there were plenty of times when I was happy. Very happy. And I wasn't grumpy now, I just didn't feel like bothering Beak Man right yet. Who knew if he was still harboring a grudge because of Evil's remark about his nose?

Eve put her hands on her hips. "Anyway, you can't stop me. If you won't come with me, I'll go alone."

Eve's voice was like a plucked violin string, all twangy and hard. When she got this way, there was no stopping her. "Oh, all right." I nodded. "It can't really hurt anything." And maybe the man would shoo her off and she'd learn a lesson.

I followed her into the corridor. Eve went right to the next compartment and lifted her knuckles to knock. I caught her hand before it touched the door. "See the sign?" I whispered. With my other hand I tilted Eve's head down toward the DO NOT DISTURB sign that hung from the knob.

"I won't disturb," said Eve.

"Knocking is disturbing. Come on back to our compartment."

"But all I want . . ."

"No. He probably wants to sleep. Come on." I pulled Eve back into the compartment and shut the door.

"*Kree,*" came the scream from next door. "*Kree, kree, kree.*"

"He's doing birdcalls, not sleeping." Eve stood in front of me with her arms crossed at her chest. She stuck out her bottom lip. "How would it disturb him just to knock and ask if I could join him?"

"You can't," I said, "and that's that."

Eve plopped down beside me and gave an angry huffy noise.

I waited for her to fight back. And I was ready — after all, a DO NOT DISTURB sign meant just that.

Eve hummed, and braided a small lock of hair over her left ear. "You really ought to learn how to braid, Zach. If you can braid, all the girls will like you."

"I can braid." I turned on the seat and faced her. I took a lock of hair over her right ear and started working. "And I don't just braid." I wrapped one lock around the other and made a loop. I tugged on it. "Remember, I was a Cub Scout. See? I do a sailor's knot and a sheepshank and a hangman's noose and . . ."

Eve pulled her hair out of my hands and unknotted it. I had managed to tangle it pretty bad. Her mouth scrunched up in concentration. "Sometimes you stink, Mister Grump." She looked out the window.

I thought maybe I'd get some peace now — Eve was mad enough to leave me alone for a while. I picked up my book and opened it again.

Someone knocked at our door.

Eve jumped up and opened it.

The conductor was a stubby man with a pointed beard. Sort of like Humpty-Dumpty in this old book we used to look at when we were little. He handed Eve two tickets. "Dinner at six-thirty." He made a check on the list in his hand.

"Can we go now?" asked Eve.

"Not yet. Hope you enjoy it." The conductor left.

Eve sighed loudly. "Well, he certainly wasn't very chatty." That's what Mom always called Eve — "chatty" — it reminded me of a chipmunk. Eve clutched the tickets and waved them in my face. "All these tickets have printed on them is six-thirty. That doesn't seem very smart. What's to keep us from using them at six-thirty in the morning? They should at least say 'dinner.'"

I yawned and kept reading.

Eve sighed again. "We just crossed over a river and it was entirely dry."

I looked out the window, but of course, the river was past already. "Like the Todd River bed that we rode camels down on Saturday." Mom

had taken us on a lot of hokey tourist things —
and the camel ride was one of the best.

"That was a riverbed? Oh." Eve laughed. "I
wondered why it was all low and sandy with so
few bushes." She sat down again with her hands
together in her lap, clutching the tickets. "I have
a Violet Crumble in my pack. You think we
should eat it? I mean, it is before dinner, but
we're starving."

A Violet Crumble is an Australian candy bar
with chocolate on the outside and a sort of hon-
eycomb, crunchy candy on the inside. It sounds
better than it is. Eve insisted on eating only
Australian candy while we were here. If she'd
had a Snickers bar, I'd have said we should eat it.
"Pig, ruining your appetite with candy. Mom
would be disappointed in you."

"Oh, yeah. Mom." Eve's voice trailed off and I
detected a trace of a tremble in it. She couldn't
be missing Mom already, could she?

I looked at my watch. "Dinner's in fifteen minutes."

"Oh!" Eve jumped up. "Well, let's go."

"That's not what I meant. I just told you so
you'd have something to think about."

"Well, I'm thinking about it. So let's go."

"It's only one carriage away. And the conductor said we should wait."

"We can walk slow. I'm starving, Zach." Eve opened the door and walked out.

I took a look at myself in the mirror. My face was clean and my shirt wasn't too wrinkled yet. I looked presentable. Mom had said the dinner should be very nice — good food, in a dining room setting, with a tablecloth and real china. She had told us to act our very best. I pushed the little silver button under the mirror and filled a glass with chilled water. First class was truly something. For a second I felt like I was rich. I drank it down quick and followed Eve out into the corridor.

Eve had turned the opposite way and stopped in front of the door of Beak Man's compartment, as I thought she would. I plucked at her sleeve. "Come on."

With a sigh, she gave up and we walked together to the end of the carriage. We opened the door and stepped into the area where the two carriages joined. The walls on both sides were accordian-shaped, made of some sort of flexible plastic or rubber, and the walls of one carriage overlapped that of the next. The noise of the wheels could be heard as loud as if we were outside. It startled me.

Just as the door of our carriage closed behind us, the train lurched. The floor of our carriage jiggled to one side — the floor of the next carriage jiggled to the other side. I jumped from one platform to the next, pulling Eve behind me. I quickly opened the door of the next carriage and we went in.

"That was spooky," said Eve. "Noisy, too."

I walked ahead of her to the dining area. A porter, but not Eugene, stopped us. "We're just cleaning up from the first sitting. You can come back in ten minutes, thank you."

We walked back to the carriage door and went out into the area between the carriages again. I walked in front of Eve, like before. My hand was already on the handle of the door to our carriage when I saw Beak Man through the door window. He stood at the end of the corridor with his back toward us. He had both hands up high and he was working on something on the wall of the carriage with a screwdriver. It was a clear plastic cover over an opening. He took off the plastic cover, reached in, took something out, and put it in his pocket. Then he replaced the plastic cover and screwed it back into place.

The whole thing had taken maybe two minutes, and the whole time Eve had been struggling to get past me and into our carriage. Two minutes is a long time to balance yourself in the jiggly area between train carriages while fighting off your little sister from behind. My fencing training came in handy; I held her back without either of us falling. I didn't want Beak Man to know we had seen him. I don't really know why. I just didn't want us interrupting a man who had put a DO NOT DISTURB sign on his door. And I felt fairly certain that whatever he had just been doing, it wasn't the ordinary thing for passengers to do.

I finally turned around and forced Eve to turn around, and we came out into the dining car again.

Eve turned to me. Her face was red and her eyes were shiny and wet. "I was scared to death! Why did you do that?"

"I'm sorry." And I was. Eve looked like she was about to cry. She was annoying and babyish — but she didn't deserve to be frightened like that. I hadn't meant to frighten her. It just happened that way. "I'm really sorry, Eve. I decided not to go back into our carriage."

"Why?"

The dining porter came up to us. "Is there a problem here? Dinner will not be served for several more minutes."

"My watch broke," I said. I smiled. Then I took Eve by the hand and opened the door of the carriage.

"No." She balked like a mule. "I'm not going out there with you again."

"I'll be quick this time, I promise." I pulled her behind me and we passed fast into our carriage.

"We made it. Oh, goodie." Eve bubbled over with relief. "Let's go back to our own compartment and wait there."

I looked up. Above the little plastic cover on the wall of the carriage a sign read, EMERGENCY KEY. Beak Man had taken the emergency key. He had done it stealthily. He had stolen it. Beak Man had stolen a key.

A key to what?

We walked back to the compartment and sat inside in silence. Several times I opened my mouth to tell Eve about the stolen key, but I shut it again without a word. Eve was unpredictable. And I didn't want unpredictable things happening until I understood better what was going on. When it was precisely six-thirty, I said, "Let's go."

I opened the compartment door and something made me look to the right — even though the dining car was to the left. Beak Man had stepped out of his compartment, followed by another man. The second man was medium height, medium weight, with a medium-sized nose, in medium clothes. I wondered if Beak Man had chosen him as a buddy because he couldn't stand to be with anyone who might be as noticeable as him. Beak Man reached into his pocket and leaned over the handle on his compartment door.

"Just a minute," Eve called from inside our compartment.

Beak Man looked sideways at me with annoyance on his face, as though I'd interrupted him.

My heart jumped. I turned to Eve and closed the door of our compartment behind me. "I thought you were starving."

"I am. But look." She had discovered the button for chilled water. She filled a glass and drank it down slowly. "It's so luxurious, Zach. Wouldn't it be wonderful to be rich?"

I wanted to say something snide to put her off, but I'd been thinking the same thing myself not so long ago. I nodded.

She smiled. "Okay, I'm ready now."

I opened the door again and peeked. The corridor was empty. We went out and closed the door. It didn't lock. We had no key for it, anyway. I bent over and looked at the place where a key would go. Instead of a keyhole, there was a square lug.

Eve headed for the dining car.

I walked quickly in the other direction to Beak Man's compartment and tried the handle. It wouldn't move: Beak Man's compartment was locked. I inspected the key spot. It was a square lug, identical to ours.

I hurried after Eve.

Eve heard my running steps. She stopped and turned. "Did you forget something?" She came toward me.

I was even with the compartment on the other side of ours, now. I pulled on the handle. The door swung open and a woman in her slip looked at me with a dumbfounded face. "Sorry." I closed the door quickly.

"What are you doing?" Eve's eyes were huge. "Look what you did."

"It was a mistake. Let's go to dinner." But it wasn't a mistake. I didn't try the next compartment down because I knew it wasn't locked. None of the compartments was locked. None but the very last compartment of the carriage — our neighbors' compartment. That's what the emergency key was for — it locked and unlocked the compartments. All of them. They all had identical square lugs on the door handles. Why had our neighbors stolen the key? To lock their compartment, of course. But why? What did they have that was so valuable they had to lock it away? And why couldn't they just have asked the porter Eugene for a key? If they had something valuable, surely Eugene would have given them a key, wouldn't he?

We passed through the doors and into the dining car without a word. The dining room steward seated us. He handed us each a menu and left. I stared at the menu. Eve had been right — chicken was one of the choices. I would have wondered how she knew, except I couldn't stop thinking about the stolen key.

"Smile, Zach." Eve whispered into my ear, "It's okay. The woman doesn't know who you are. She's not here at dinner. And if you ever see her again, you can pretend you don't know her. Please smile."

I looked at my crazy little sister. "What woman?"

"The woman in the slip."

"Oh, of course." I nodded. Eve was trying to make me feel better. How strange. Sometimes she could be almost nice. The funny part was, I didn't feel bad at all. I had completely forgotten about the dumb woman in the slip. So Eve was being nice to me when I didn't even need it.

"You're right. Thanks. Let's pick our dinners."

"I want chicken. Oh, look. The ballerina clown is sitting over there. And he's got a friend. I'm going to ask him about birdcalls."

"Later, Eve. Let him eat now, okay?"

"Okay." Eve twirled her dolphin mood ring around on her finger. Mom had bought it for her in Cairns. It was too big for her, but she wore it all the time anyway. It was bright purple right now. It was almost always purple. Purple meant you were happy. I wondered what color it would be if I wore it?

CHAPTER 3

Birdcalls

Eve rolled her cherry tomato around her dinner plate. I watched her, knowing I should tell her to eat it but not feeling like starting up again. She'd think I was picking on her, instead of looking out for her. Yup, she'd fight for sure. Eve had been mad at me ever since Beak Man and his medium friend had left the dining car and I wouldn't let her follow them. I had decided to avoid them as much as possible. So my not letting her follow them was another instance of looking out for her. But she would never see it that way.

Eve caught me looking at the tomato. "When I eat tomatoes, I turn red," she said.

I refused to answer. Anything I said would encourage her.

"If I ate this tomato and my hair turned green, I'd look like a big tomato walking around with feet." She flicked the tomato like you flick a marble, and it flew off our table and rolled under the table across the aisle. "I don't want to eat tomatoes anymore." She picked up her fork and smashed around in her custard cup. "And dessert stinks."

I didn't say anything about the tomato under the other table, or about the mess she was making of her custard. I wouldn't be drawn into a fight no matter what she did. I wasn't looking for a fight, really I wasn't. Plus, I hated fighting in public.

Eve wiped her nose on the back of her hand. "You're mean not to ever let me make new friends."

"If you've finished with your dessert," said the dining room steward, looking at my empty plate and Eve's mashed flat custard blob, "there's a children's video starting in the Entertainment Car in a few minutes."

Eve perked up. "What's the movie?"

"I don't recall the title exactly. Something about three men and a young woman. Children like it."

"We've seen it," I said.

"We can see it again." Eve stood up. "Come on, Zach."

I hadn't liked the movie the first time around and I wasn't about to watch it a second time. But I wasn't sure Eve should go by herself. Anyway, there were other things to do in the Entertainment Car, according to the brochure in our compartment. I could keep busy while Eve watched.

The Entertainment Car turned out to be several sleeper carriages away from us. I searched the faces of everyone we passed on the way. Beak Man and his medium buddy were nowhere around. I relaxed a little.

When we got there, two kids were already watching the screen. There were three empty seats. Eve grabbed one and watched as though this was the best video she'd ever seen. I wandered away and discovered a tiny souvenir shop at the end of the carriage. It was empty except for the clerk.

The clerk couldn't have been more than eighteen or nineteen. He smiled at me in a friendly way. "What can I do for you, mate?"

I liked the way he called me mate, as though we were buddies. It made me feel older. "I'm just looking around." I gestured toward where I'd left Eve. "Passing time while my sister watches a movie."

"You're not Australian, are you?"

"American."

"Well, look at that. I thought we had no foreigners on the train tonight." The clerk took out a notebook and flipped it open. He looked like he was ready to forget about me.

"I'm from Philadelphia." Actually, I'm from Swarthmore, outside Philly. But I found that Australians didn't even know Philadelphia, so there was no point in getting more precise than that.

The clerk kept his eyes in his notebook. "Never heard of it."

"About two hours south of New York."

"Oh, yeah?" He looked up from the notebook. "I have a cousin that visited New York. You must find Australia pretty boring after New York."

"Australia's not boring at all." I thought about all the things we'd done and seen in the past ten days. "We don't have kangaroos all around us where I live."

"Well, we've got plenty of them here, all right." He leaned over the counter and pointed out the window behind me into the darkening evening. "Just keep your eyes open and you're bound to see some kangaroos or wallabies hopping about before it gets too dark out."

I looked out into the gloom. We zipped by a junked car. "How'd a car get way out here?"

"A dirt road runs alongside, for the gangs that work on the tracks. There's a lot of those old cars. It's almost like an extended tip."

"What's a tip?" I asked.

"A place where you throw old stuff."

"A dump," I said half to myself. It was awful to think of the desert filled with junked cars. But no one lived out here — and the animals probably didn't care. Still, it made me sad. We passed a tall structure with four steel legs and a satellite dish on top and a little cement house beside it. The steel legs were taller than a telephone pole. Much taller. And halfway up an array of metal rods stuck out, vertical and parallel to each other. "What was that?"

"Radio tower."

"Radio?" I imagined a radio announcer alone in the tower talking over the air to no one, gradually losing his mind from loneliness. "Who listens to the radio way out here?"

The guy laughed. "Not radio stations. It's for talking between the trains and the train stations along the track."

"I thought the Ghan was the only train that went between Alice Springs and Adelaide."

"It's the only passenger train, but there are lots of freight trains. A few each day."

A man came in right then and picked up a tee shirt with a picture of a camel on it and THE GHAN written in big letters. The man was tall and bald, with fat cheeks, and he looked sort of camel-like himself. I didn't think the shirt was the best choice for him. On the other hand, the shirt he had on had XXXX on the chest. That's the sign of one of Australia's beers. I recognized it because in all the towns we'd been to, beer was advertised. The Australians love their beer and Mom said they had every reason to. The shirt matched the man's belly, which was unflattering to say the least — maybe the camel shirt was actually an improvement for him. He plunked a twenty-dollar bill on the counter. The clerk said, "Thank you," gave him his change, and turned back to me. "Most sidings have a radio tower on the west side of the tracks."

"What's a siding?"

The clerk looked at me as though I were a half-wit. "A siding, you know, where there are two sets of tracks so one train can pull over and let another one pass. There's only a single track the full distance, so if a freight train comes along, either we pull over at the loop in the tracks or they do. Whoever gets there first."

I nodded. "What's the satellite dish for? I mean, radio waves don't need them."

"Trackers." He leaned toward me and spoke in a lower voice. "Ever heard of Pine Gap?"

I shook my head.

"It's a USA top security station." He hesitated for effect, then he added, "Top secret. They used it in the Gulf War to track satellites. Right here in Australia, they did." He looked around, then he leaned closer. "We already passed it, though, or I would have pointed it out to you. It's near the Finke River, which is dried out this time of year, of course, but after a northern storm it runs in a wall of water. It's the oldest river in the world." He stood up proudly. "The very oldest."

I wondered how people could figure out the age of a river. But I didn't ask. I didn't want him to think I didn't believe him.

"Those towers come in handy in emergencies." He nodded emphatically. "We get some pretty interesting emergencies."

"Oh, yeah?"

"Like once we got the message that a Japanese man who had rented a motorbike didn't get back to his tour — and he only had enough water for two days. So we were told to look out for him, and, sure enough, we picked him up. Probably saved the guy's life. You get dehydrated in the desert fast."

"Did he look awful when you found him?"

The clerk turned red. "Well, I said, 'we,' but I wasn't actually on the train that time. We travel a lot of routes. I don't do this particular route more than about once every other week."

"I've got a great joke!" Eve appeared beside me and smiled her charmer smile at the clerk. The clerk smiled back, clearly charmed. I hadn't even heard her come up. Eve was like that; she could come out of nowhere and destroy every bit of peace I had anytime she wanted.

"Go back to your movie," I whispered.

"I already saw it," she hissed back.

"You tell terrible jokes," I whispered.

"I didn't make up this one," said Eve. "The kid sitting beside me at the movie told me." She looked at the clerk, who was leaning forward across the counter, obviously delighted at the idea of a joke. "What do you call a green thing that sits in the corner?"

The clerk ran his tongue around inside his cheek and looked at Eve with a twinkle in his eye. "What?"

"A naughty frog."

The clerk looked at me, clearly baffled. Good for him.

I looked at Eve in annoyance.

She grinned. "What do you call a white thing that sits in the corner?"

We both looked at her.

"A naughty fridge!" Eve doubled over in laughter.

I tapped her on the shoulder. "Let's go." I looked at the clerk sheepishly. "Good-night."

He waved us off. "Cheerio for now."

"Cheerio," called Eve.

Once we were out of his hearing distance, I let her have it. "Why'd you have to go and ruin things? We were talking."

"You wouldn't let me talk to my friend."

"What friend?"

"The ballerina man."

"Beak Man isn't your friend."

"Beak Man? Is that what you call him?" Eve giggled. "Oh, I forgot my candy. I've got to go back."

"Forget it. Violet Crumble is yuck."

"No, this is different candy. A kid gave me some. And I left them on the chair."

"Forget it," I said. "Let's go."

"No!" Eve turned and headed for the movie place.

"Well, I'm not waiting for you. You can just get to our carriage by yourself." That ought to have done it. I knew she'd be scared to walk from one carriage to the next without me after our experience before dinner.

But Eve didn't hesitate. She ran off.

I went back to our carriage, counting the carriages between. There were seven all together. Eve would die of fright before she got back, and it served her right. Evil with her dumb jokes. Evil, who could walk into anyplace anytime and get everyone to pay attention to her.

When I got in our compartment, I found a piece of Ghan stationery in the folder on my bed. (Eugene must have come in and swung our bunkbeds down from the wall while we were at dinner.) I wrote, "Dead Man — Do Not Disturb." I opened the door and closed the edge of the note into the door, so that it would stay perched right above the door handle. That would really get Eve good.

Next, I studied the shower. It looked doable. So I risked it. It was actually hot and quite refreshing. I put on a sweat suit and sat on the bottom bunk, Eve's bunk, to wait for her. We didn't sleep in sweat suits at home, but since we'd been traveling, we'd found it made sense. During the day the temperature could rise enough that shorts and a short-sleeve shirt felt fine. But at night the thermometer plummeted, especially here in the desert. So Mom had bought us nice sweats, with pockets and an elastic waist, instead of a drawstring — that way they could double as outfits to go out in at night. Still, the train turned out to be heated, unlike our hotel in Alice Springs, and I already felt a little hot.

I waited.

We passed another junked car, turned over and stripped of its tires.

I waited.

The desert was vast. Endless.

Like this waiting.

What could be keeping the little dork?

She couldn't be in any kind of trouble. There wasn't any trouble to get into on this train.

Unless she was stuck back in the Entertainment Car, afraid to go through the passage between the carriages. But even then, she wouldn't really be in trouble. She'd just ask some stranger to help her. Eve never hesitated to talk to strangers.

Eve never hesitated to talk to strangers. The idea made me suddenly cold. I got up and opened the door. Eve better be all right. My sign fluttered down to the floor of the corridor. And there, standing with their backs to the window, chatting together, were Eve and Beak Man. She'd done it again — just like when the train first pulled out of Alice Springs. My mouth dropped open. I closed it fast.

"A butcherbird," said Eve, loudly, "didn't you hear me?"

"You do it," said the man.

Eve did the butcherbird call that the Aborigine had taught her in Alice Springs yesterday. The man looked bored. "Can you do that?" asked Eve.

Beak Man shook his head.

Eve frowned. "How about a galah call?"

"Galah?" He screwed up his mouth and looked like he was concentrating.

"Galah," said Eve a little louder. "Galah." She looked frustrated. "I know that's what they're called. The pink and gray parrots."

"Oh, yeah, them."

Eve looked puzzled. "Galahs are all over the place. Everyone knows a galah. You were just joking, right?"

"Sure," said Beak Man. "I've got to go in now. And it looks like your best mate wants to put you to bed." He gave me a curt nod and went into his compartment.

I held the door of our compartment open and Eve came in. I looked at her with murder in my eyes, feeling as far from a best mate as anyone ever had, I'm sure. I shut the door. "You shouldn't have stood alone in the corridor talking to him."

"Why not?" Eve sat down on her bunk and pulled a handful of wrapped candies from her pocket.

"You know very well why not. You're not stupid."

"See?" Eve grinned at me. "You admitted it."

"Well, you are stupid," I said, "but you still know better than to talk to strange men alone."

Eve unwrapped a chocolate cube. "Have one, there's caramel inside." She handed me the candy and smoothed the wrapping out on her lap. "Listen, there's writing on the wrappers. Who do you want to hear about? Kylie Minogue or Nicole Kidman? They're both Australian stars."

I chewed the candy without answering. It was pretty good.

Eve unwrapped another candy. "Here are some American ones. Jeff Bridges and Meryl Streep."

I picked up the wrapper she'd discarded. The candy was called Fantales, and the wrapper had all sorts of information about movie stars. "Meryl Streep," I said.

"Sorry, I can't tell you about her 'cause it's cut off at the bottom."

"Why'd you offer, then?" I said irritably.

"Michael Douglas was born on September 25, 1944. Hey, isn't that the year Mom was born?"

"It's the year millions of people were born. And died."

Eve crumpled the wrapper quickly and looked at me with a determined face. "Zach, there's something wrong about the ballerina man."

I wondered if she knew about the key. "What makes you say that?" I asked, trying to keep the excitement out of my voice.

"We heard that cockatoo scream just as clear

as day. But when I asked him to make birdcalls, he couldn't make a single one."

"So maybe his friend made the birdcall."

"He said his friend doesn't know any birdcalls, either."

I thought about that. "Maybe he just didn't want you bothering them anymore."

Eve shook her head.

Someone knocked on our door.

Eve moved closer to me. I was surprised at her edginess. I rubbed the back of her hand like Mom rubs mine when she wants to comfort me. "Who is it?" I called out.

"Eugene."

I opened the door.

Eugene looked around the compartment with satisfaction. "Everything okay here?"

"Yes," I said.

"Then I won't peek in on you again till the morning. Have a pleasant night's sleep." He shut the door.

I looked out the window. It was really dark now. We passed another radio tower.

"What was that?" said Eve.

"A radio tower."

"What was that on top?"

"A satellite dish. There are American satellite tracking stations all over Australia," I said.

"How'd you know that?"

"Everyone knows that."

Eve was silent.

I felt guilty; after all, I hadn't known that till the clerk told me. And I was annoyed at myself. I knew exactly why I'd said that. Eve knew too many things I didn't know — like which parrots were galahs. It bugged me. I was the big brother. Why did she always have to pipe up with all those facts? I stared out into the blackness with the heavy heart of a liar. I wished we'd see a kangaroo right then so Eve would be happy.

"*Kree!*" came the call from the other side of the wall.

Eve sat perfectly still. I could feel her stillness beside me. I could feel her sadness. Maybe she was missing Mom already. I sort of missed Mom myself. A night away from Mom in a strange country. Maybe I should get Eve to take her shower and get ready for bed. I turned to her, just in time to see her disappear out the compartment door. I ran after her. But before I could

stop her, she had opened Beak Man's compartment door. She didn't even knock. She just went
inside and left the door open behind her. I followed, apologies already on my tongue.

But the compartment was empty. The men
had gone out and forgotten to lock it. Eve was
on the floor by the cage. She lifted the black
cloth and the huge black bird inside screamed,
"Kree, kree, kree." It blinked its round, shiny eyes.

The men stepped into the compartment behind us and shut the door.

CHAPTER 4

Big Mistake

"I knew it was a real bird." Eve stood up. She smiled at Beak Man, but it wasn't her normal dumbbell smile. She chewed her bottom lip nervously. We were trespassers and even Eve knew these men had a right to be angry. "I think birds aren't supposed to be in the compartments," she said in a half-perky voice.

I looked at Eve as though she were demented. What did she think she was doing, scolding the men like that, when we had no right to even be in their compartment? But then I recognized the trick. She did it to me with Mom all the time. Whenever she did something terrible to me, she'd talk about some different thing I'd done — totally justified, of course — to deflect Mom's anger. Only Mom wasn't in charge here now. And I didn't think that tactic was going to work with Beak Man. All I wanted was to apologize and get out of there fast. But Eve didn't know about the stolen compartment key. She didn't know Beak Man had worked hard to keep his compartment private. So Eve wasn't as worried as I was; she was mostly just embarrassed.

"I saw a woman get on the train with a dog in a cage, and they took it away from her. It was a little dog. A poodle, I think." Eve's nervousness was making her run off at the mouth. "I mean I'm glad you have the bird in here, but . . ."

I moved in front of Eve. "Sorry to have bothered you. We have to go now." I took her by the hand and stepped toward the door.

Beak Man and his medium buddy blocked the way. "Sit down," said Beak Man.

I held Eve's hand tight and kept standing. It looked like they needed another apology. Well, that was fine. I was about as sorry as I could be. "Look, it won't happen again. I . . ."

"Sit down!"

We sat on the bench and I prepared myself to listen to a lecture on trespassing. Probably a loud lecture. My stomach tied in knots. The bunks in this compartment weren't folded down yet. I thought of Eugene coming to the compartment to prepare it while we were all at dinner and finding the door locked. Had he been surprised? Had he reported it? Who would he report something like that to? Then I remembered the DO NOT DISTURB sign. If they had put it on their door while they were at dinner, Eugene never would have tried the door. He wouldn't ever have found out it was locked. For some reason that thought made me feel queasy and heavy. It was as though everything was slowing down. Why didn't Beak Man just get on with his lecture so we could go back to our compartment? At least Eve was silent. That was something to be grateful for. She sat close beside me with her hand still in mine.

"Hey, what's going on?" Beak Man frowned at the medium guy. "The train's slowing down."

"I don't feel anything." The medium guy looked out the window into the dark. "And I can't see anything, either."

"Of course you can't see anything," said Beak Man. "It's night."

"I can see at night."

"Not when you're in a lit-up room and you're looking out the window."

Their squabbling made them seem like brothers, and the idea that Beak Man and the medium guy could be brothers seemed so ridiculous I think I might have laughed if I hadn't felt so sick. And slow. And, oh, it wasn't just my insides — Beak Man was right: the train was definitely slowing down.

A little speaker high over the mirror came on. "Nothing to be alarmed about, ladies and gentlemen. There's a herd of camels ahead. We'll slow down a bit till we're safely past them. Let me take this opportunity to announce that drinks are now being served in the Dreamtime Lounge." The speaker clicked off.

The train was going along at a bicycle's pace now. I looked out the black window and half expected to see a camel's nose smush up against the pane. I knew all about them, because when we went on our camel ride in Alice Springs they told us some camels had escaped from British traders decades ago and formed wild herds that were a hazard to cars at night. They hadn't mentioned trains.

"Camels." Beak Man rubbed at the back of his neck and rotated his shoulders. He looked like he was getting ready to stretch his wings and fly away. For a moment I wondered how a gangly bird like him could have made me so worried.

"What were you doing snooping around in here?" said the medium guy gruffly, quickly making me stop wondering. He had obviously just decided to try intimidation, but he came across as big and stupid, like a bear. On the other hand, I didn't feel much like dealing with a big, stupid bear. Plus, he had a right to be angry.

I sat up straight and tried to let my body convey the message that I wasn't a little kid they could just order around. We'd talked about body language in health class last year. If your body looks like a victim, that invites a bully. "Nothing. We weren't doing anything."

"We're not snoops," said Eve with a sniff.

I looked at her, stunned. Obviously, my body language message had gotten through to her loud and clear. She didn't realize I was bluffing, so here she was, taking a cue from me and acting indignant. Indignant, of all things. Of course we were snoops. Or, rather, she was a snoop. The worst kind of snoop. I had simply tried to stop her.

"Let me handle this," said Beaky. "You've done enough damage."

"Huh?" said Bear Breath. "What'd I do?" He thrust his jaw forward belligerently.

Beaky gave a sarcastic little laugh. "Going to the gambling car was your idea."

"No one forced you to come along," said Bear Breath. He was clever at quick responses.

Beaky opened his mouth to answer. Then he shook his head as if in disgust. He turned to Eve and forced a smile. "All right, missy. So animals go in the brake van with the luggage. But if you had a big black bird like this one, would you put it in with the luggage? Would you really? The brake van isn't heated."

"This bird is native to this area," said Eve. "He's used to the cold nights." She wiggled a little in her seat and I could tell she was congratulating herself for her answer. I wondered if she actually expected them to say how smart she was.

And I was truly impressed at her denseness; she had no idea we were in a tight spot.

Beaky's smile strained. "It's dark and noisy in the brake van. There's no moonlight even. Would you really put a bird like this in a dark, noisy brake van?"

Eve lifted her chin defiantly. I squeezed her hand. This wasn't a moment for another wise-guy answer. I squeezed hard. Eve shook her head slowly. "No. He'd get so scared, he'd probably die." She glanced at me briefly, then she looked up at Beaky with a blank expression. I stopped squeezing. She pulled her hand away and folded her hands in her lap. "Birds aren't like dogs, you're right. But if you asked Eugene, I bet he'd let you keep the bird in the compartment." Defiance crept back into her voice. "That way you wouldn't have to sneak around." She empha-sized the word *sneak*. I could tell she wanted to get back at them for calling us snoops.

Beaky kept that thin smile on his face. "Against regulations. No exceptions, missy. No animals of any sort are allowed in the compart-ments." He leaned toward Eve and winked. That one gesture worried me more than anything else so far. It was sinister. A sense of urgency rose inside me. "Health, you know," said Beaky, "and disturbance to the other passengers."

"Well, that explains that," I said cheerily. "Time to go." Oh boy, was it time to go! I stood up.

Beaky stood with his toes touching mine. My face was pointed at the middle of his chest. "Have a seat." His voice wasn't friendly. I sat down again. "Wouldn't you children like a bedtime treat? I have some biscuits here." He pulled down a carry bag from the overhead rack. A woman's nylon stocking floated down. It had a black feather caught in it and a lump of bird dropping smeared on the inside.

Eve's mouth opened in a gasp.

I pinched her thigh. If these men wanted to carry that bird around in a nylon stocking, that was okay with us. After all, they had to restrain it while they snuck it on board, right? It wasn't cruel to the bird. Well, I don't know. Maybe it was cruel to the bird. But it wasn't our business. Well, maybe it was our business. Maybe cruelty to animals is everyone's business. But one thing was sure, there wasn't a thing we could do about it. Not right then, anyway. I cleared my throat and shook my head at the tin of cookies. "We ate a lot of dinner." I kept my tone polite and my voice strong. "We have to go now. We won't tell Eugene about the bird," I lied. "Or anyone else." I stood up again. That should have done the trick.

It didn't. Beaky pushed me in the chest. I sat back down. I felt like a jack-in-the-box. Beaky dropped the tin by my feet. I read the label. Shortbread cookies with apricot centers. Didn't sound too bad. I might have eaten a dozen if I didn't feel like puking.

"That stocking . . . ," said Eve in a shaky voice. I could feel the mix of emotions seething inside her. I wished she hadn't seen the stocking. There were few people I knew who could match Eve for indignant self-righteousness. Maybe few in the world. Her arm trembled beside mine. But she shut up. I realized she was finally afraid. Only fear could keep Eve silent.

Bear Breath picked up the stocking and jammed it in his pocket. I had to hand it to him: he was clever at quick actions, too. What a do-do. And I realized I was focusing on his stupidity so that I wouldn't focus on his size and strength. My mouth went dry with fear.

Eve cleared her throat. No, I thought. Please, Eve, don't talk. But she didn't hear my silent message. "That cage is way too small for a bird that size." Her voice came out like a brittle spike. All the cockiness was gone. She was being a brave little soldier, expecting full well to get scolded for it, but rising to defend truth and justice. She was proud of herself. But I couldn't be proud of her. All I wanted was for her to swallow her anger and pride and let us get out of there safely. If these men could stuff a bird in a stocking, I didn't want to know their idea of proper discipline for trespassing children.

Beaky said, "Ha ha," as though he thought we'd really think he was laughing. "That's just his transport cage. He stays in a large cage at home. It's so big, I can walk in it."

"Good," said Eve. Her voice shook. "A cockatoo needs plenty of space." She looked down and hesitated. I could tell she was considering saying something more, but whatever it was made her think twice. And if Eve thought what she was about to say was worth thinking twice over, then it was probably a real killer. Eve was about to plunge us into serious trouble. I pinched her thigh again, harder this time. She moved her leg away. Why was I condemned to having Evil for a sister? Her high voice was hard to hear. "You really keep it in your home? I thought it was against the law to keep this kind of bird. Only zoos and sanctuaries can keep them."

"Don't be silly, Eve," I said, with an ingratiating smile at the men. Beaky watched me attentively, but Bear Breath stood with his mouth open. He wasn't even like a bear. It was as though he had no brains at all. I cleared my throat and chided Eve. "Even those friends of Mom's in Alice Springs had a cockatoo." I stood up, looking at Eve with what I hoped appeared to be big-brotherly reproach. "Let's not bother these men anymore. We have to go now."

Beaky pushed me in the chest again. I teetered and fell back onto the bench. Jack-in-the-box strikes again.

"That was a sulphur-crested cockatoo," said Eve simply. The girl had no idea when to shut up. "Not a black cockatoo. Not a red-tailed black cockatoo like this one." She looked at me with sincerity, as though convincing me was more important than anything else in the world. My sister had fatal stupidity.

No Brains's eyebrows came together in one big ugly lump over his nose. "He's a palm cockatoo."

"No he's not," said Eve in a calm, tiny voice. No one could tell Eve which bird was which. She spent hours every day looking in her bird books. No Brains didn't know what he was up against, the big, dumb clunk.

"Yes he is!" No Brains pulled a piece of paper out of his pocket and read from it. "Black all over, tall black crest, red markings." He folded the piece of paper and stuck it back in his pocket. He looked defiantly at Eve. "That's a palm cockatoo, all right."

"The red marks on a palm cockatoo are on his face, not on his tail," said Eve. She twisted her dolphin mood ring around on her finger. It was blue now. What emotion did blue signify? "And his crest is really tall, much taller than the red-tailed cockatoo's crest. It looks royal. I have a couple of pictures of him in my compartment if you want to see." Eve's voice cracked. "One in my bird book and one on my medallion."

I remembered Eve's medallion. We were in the bank with Mom and Eve spied a brochure about endangered species in Australia and there was a bird on the list. Next thing I knew, Mom went and bought Eve a commemorative medallion of the bird — the money went to save it from extinction. So her medallion bird was a palm cockatoo.

"The palm cockatoo is endangered," said Eve softly. "But the black cockatoo is in trouble, too. It's a protected species today."

I swallowed the lump in my throat. These men were sneaking around with a protected species in a cage. And they thought it was a palm cockatoo, so they thought they were sneaking around with an endangered species. Either way it was illegal. They were criminals. Incompetent ones, maybe, but still criminals. We were sitting in a compartment with criminals. I could call No Brains any number of funny names in my head, but no amount of funny names would make him funny really. This was way beyond funny. I stood up quickly and stepped as hard as I could on Beaky's feet as I did it.

"Ouch!" He stepped back instinctively.

I had Eve by the hand and I rushed for the door.

No Brains blocked my path.

Eve screamed.

It was as though her scream was the cue. The bird squawked so loud my ears rang. Someone laid a giant noisy fart. I shouted, "Help!" Where was Eugene right now? Wasn't anyone coming back from dinner and walking in the corridor? If we hadn't been in the last compartment of the carriage, someone would have heard us for sure. Wasn't anyone anywhere going to hear us? I had a sudden image of everyone sitting around the Dreamtime Lounge, laughing and swapping camel stories.

No Brains pinned me from behind and had the stocking around my open, shouting mouth within seconds. It was so tight, I thought the corners of my mouth would rip and my tongue would get cut in half. Beaky held his hand over Eve's mouth. Eve bit him. He reached into his carry bag and pulled out a pair of socks and stuffed them into her mouth. I wondered suddenly and irrelevantly if they were clean or dirty.

He held her tight against him and his face was worried.

"Don't use the stocking!" barked Beaky. Exactly my thought — it was full of bird droppings. "We'll need it when we get off the train." Beaky gestured toward his carry bag with his shoulder. "Take a shirt or something."

No Brains pushed me along to the carry bag and let go of my mouth long enough to grab a shirt. I shouted. He stuffed part of the shirt in my mouth and tied the arms around my head. I tasted blood. The nylon must have cut me. Maybe I was dying. No Brains's hand was very big. How could anybody have hands that big? He kicked at the back of my calves. It hurt. I guessed I wasn't dead yet. His voice was loud in my left ear. "No! You think the girl's right? You think it's not a palm cockatoo?"

"So what if it isn't?" said Beaky. "It's still a black cockatoo."

"I said we shouldn't do birds. I said . . ."

"Shut up!" Beaky jerked Eve around. She winced in pain. I tried to kick Beaky, but only managed to twist enough that No Brains squashed me harder. "It's a black cockatoo. That's enough," said Beaky. "They want us to keep running this route for them, they'll accept it. They'll have to. The thing we got to do now is deal with these kids."

"I said we shouldn't do birds. The first bird was easy, okay. But I knew something bad would happen sooner or later. I said . . ."

"Shut up!" shouted Beaky.

"We should have stuck to fossils," muttered No Brains. "Fossils don't make noises that bring people nosing around. And there's always a market for fossils."

"We'll still do fossils," said Beaky. His voice was full of determination. "But there's big money in birds. You've seen that already. Once we know more about it, we'll handle the bird side fine." He smiled at No Brains. He actually smiled. "Come on. Let's think about getting rid of these kids."

"I'll take care of that," said No Brains. I imagined him pounding us to death with his big, meaty hands.

"No." Beaky shook his head. He'd probably had the same image I'd had. He'd defend us now.

He had to. He had a brain in his head. A bird brain, maybe, but a brain. These men were thieves. Bird thieves. But stealing wasn't that bad a crime. I mean it wasn't murder. And it wasn't kidnapping. So our knowing about what they'd done wasn't that serious. Not really. It wasn't worth hurting us over. Never. It would be much much worse for them if they got caught hurting us than if they got caught stealing. They had to know that. They'd talk it over and threaten us till they were sure we'd keep our mouths shut, which is what I'd promised them in the first place. I had lied, of course, but they didn't know that. "No," said Beaky again.

I waited for the debate to begin.

No Brains apparently anticipated the same debate I did. "We've got to do something. The girl here . . ."

"I'm thinking."

That's it, I said silently, cheering Beaky on.

"Look," pleaded No Brains, "I got too much at risk . . ."

"Shut up!"

Hooray, I thought, the fight is on. And Beaky will win.

79

"No," said No Brains, in a threatening voice. "You give too many orders."

"Listen," said Beaky, all chummy with No Brains again. "It's got to look like an accident."

An accident? No!

"Sure." The relief in No Brains's voice was as palpable as the cold fear in my stomach. "I can make it look . . ."

"Shut up," said Beaky. "I'm thinking." He looked around the compartment. "Those blankets up there. We can wrap the kids up and toss them off the train. No one will realize they're gone till the morning. By the time anyone finds them, we'll be long gone off this train and everyone will think they just did some stupid kid thing and wound up falling out the train."

What kind of stupid kid thing could anyone do to fall out a train, I thought. But I was in no position to say anything. It was all I could do to keep breathing with a shirt stuffed halfway down my throat and an arm crushing my chest. This was all Mom's fault. I'd told her to let me take that aikido class, but she said I had to wait till I was fourteen. Now maybe I'd never turn fourteen. My nose stung. I knew I was about to cry.

"Okay," said No Brains. "Let's drag them. We can force them out through the joining walls between the carriages."

"Wait," said Beaky. "Someone might see. I have a better idea. As soon as the train starts to pick up speed again, we'll toss them out the window."

"Uh, how do you open the window?" No Brains's words were slow. I think his own stupidity was getting to him.

"There's an emergency pull up there."

I looked at the top of the window. The emergency pull was red. My heart speeded up. That pull was connected to an alarm, I knew it. It just had to be. No Brains would pull the window open and the alarm would go off and the conductors would come bursting in and we'd be saved. I looked at Eve. Her eyes were wild with fear. I tried to tell her with my eyes to be calm, but it didn't work. Her face stayed ashen.

"Uhhh," said No Brains, "what if an alarm goes off?" I couldn't believe it — No Brains was pretending to have brains. I blinked and blinked, but a tear managed to escape anyway. It rolled down my cheek and got absorbed by the shirt.

"You're right." Beaky rocked with the train's slow, jerky motion. I thought of the cut-open paw paw rocking in our compartment. I couldn't remember if it had still been there when we came back from dinner. Maybe Eugene had cleaned it up. And a wave of nausea washed over me as I realized the train's velocity was increasing a little bit every second. "We have to throw them off at the end of the carriage. It's only a few steps from our compartment, anyway. We'll go together, as fast as we can."

I fought with every ounce of strength I had, ignoring the whacks and kicks. Within moments I found myself wrapped up tight in a blanket with the shirt pressed ever tighter around my head. I couldn't hear anything from Eve. I still twisted and threw myself around on the off chance that someone might notice us. I felt myself being carried at a run. I was hot and there was no air inside the blanket. I was definitely halfway toward being dead already. Then the noise of the wheels was loud and I was pressed on all sides and I was flying through the air.

CHAPTER 5

B o o m

Roll. Everyone knows that's what you're supposed to do when you fall or jump from something that's moving. But it's hard to roll when you're wrapped up tight in a blanket. So I kicked and flailed, with the idea that I'd roll as stage two. But I hit the ground before I got to stage two.

Somehow I had managed to get my head free of both the blanket and the shirt, so my mouth was open as I hit the sand. The breath got knocked out of me, what breath was left. A burning sensation shot up my chest. I would have screamed if I didn't have a mouth full of sand. I turned my head to one side and spit out sand and did a mental scan of my body, which seemed to be all there. It was pure luck that the train hadn't been going very fast yet when they threw us.

Us. Where was Eve? Probably suffocating to death somewhere nearby, a mass of broken bones. I kicked my way out of the blanket, relieved to find that both legs still worked, and tried to stand up. I wound up on all fours, dizzy and sick. I vomited.

"Zach! Oh, Zach, there you are!"

I looked up and saw Eve stagger toward me in the moonlight. Her skirt was ripped, but besides that she looked okay. I was about to say something clever when I vomited again.

Eve patted me on the back. "I couldn't see you at first. It was awful. I kept expecting camels to trample me."

I spit several times to get the taste of vomit out of my mouth. I shouldn't have eaten the custard at dinner. I untied the shirt which had originally gagged me and now hung around my neck, all clumpy with vomit. I threw it off to the side and stood up and looked around. I couldn't spy a single camel from the herd that had made the train slow down.

Eve huddled beside me and shivered. "I'm cold."

"Is that all that's wrong with you?" My voice came out as a croak. "Are you okay? Did you get hurt?"

"No. I'm fine."

Gratitude filled me. We were both still intact. "That's so lucky."

"It wasn't luck. I rolled. That's what you're supposed to do."

I didn't answer. It didn't seem right that Eve could irritate me here, now — lost in the desert at night. But she'd done it. "Didn't they wrap you in a blanket?"

"No. They just stuffed my mouth and held me tight and threw me. It was awful. And I'm cold."

I picked up my blanket and draped it across her back. "If you'd have gotten ready for bed when I did, you'd have your sweatshirt on now and you wouldn't feel cold." I ignored the fact that I was now barefoot because I'd gotten ready for bed, while she still had her sneakers on.

"Jumper," said Eve.

"What?" Maybe her brains had been scrambled in the fall. That would be just my luck, to have an evil sister that was now crazy, too.

"Jumper. I didn't bring a sweatshirt for such a fancy train, I brought a sweater. They call *sweaters jumpers* in Australia. And *sweatshirts* are *sloppy joes*."

"Who cares!" I shouted.

"Australians," said Eve. She pulled the blanket tight around her. "You don't have to yell at me."

I thought about that. It had felt good to shout. A lot better than quaking with fear, anyway. And those seemed to be my only choices. I looked at her bleakly. Just the two of us — way out here. "Sorry."

"I have to go to the bathroom."

I remembered the fart during the struggle. I had to ask: "Did you fart in their compartment as a weapon?"

"No. I was scared and it just flew out."

"Oh." Of course. Creative farting was beyond Eve. "Okay, well, just go do what you have to do."

"What'll I use for toilet paper?"

"You're thinking about toilet paper! Here we

are, about to die of dehydration and get eaten by wild animals . . ."

"They don't have ferocious animals in Australia." Eve giggled. "Can you imagine a killer kangaroo?" She laughed loud.

I couldn't believe it. Eve actually didn't realize how much trouble we were in. Just to sober her up, I thought of reminding her about snakes, spiders, and scorpions — what Mom's travel guide called Australia's famous three venomous *s*-creatures — but suddenly I realized she wasn't laughing anymore. She was sobbing.

I put my arm around her and pulled her close. "Don't cry." I wasn't just trying to console her; if Eve cried, she'd dehydrate that much faster. I spoke with as soothing a voice as I could manage. "We just have to think straight and we'll be okay." I pulled my handkerchief out of my pocket. "Here. Use this as toilet paper, then bury it."

Eve took the handkerchief, dropped the blanket on the ground, and went off.

My handkerchief had my initials on it. I hoped no one ever found it. I looked out across the desert. There was no sign of motion anywhere.

Wait, I was wrong. A fly buzzed around my face. A fly, way out here. What on earth could attract a fly to this endless stretch of sand?

"So you've got flies, too." Eve giggled as she came up behind me. "I got one really good."

I refused to consider the fate of Evil's fly. "I've got a plan."

Eve picked up my blanket, wrapped it around her, and looked at me with a ready face. All trace of fear was gone, just like that. In that moment I realized for the first time how much Eve trusted me. Despite all our fights, I was her big brother. I knew best. Everything was always maddeningly simple for Eve. The responsibility was enormous for me. Her life rested in my hands. Both of our lives did.

I straightened the blanket across her shoulders. "We'll walk to the nearest siding and get help at the radio tower."

Eve nodded slowly. I was sure she didn't know what a siding was. Still, she didn't ask. She wouldn't give me the satisfaction of asking. Good old stubborn Evil. For once I was grateful for her spunk. She would need it tonight.

"The radio towers are tall," I said. "We can look up and down the tracks to spot one."

Eve obediently followed me onto the tracks.

The moonlight was bright and the land was flat, so we could see a long way. That made the view that much more disheartening: there was no radio tower in sight.

Eve looked at me. "I vote we go in the direction the train went. At least that way we'll be getting closer to where we want to go."

Where we wanted to go was anywhere people were — fast, before the lack of water got to us. But I didn't say that. For once in my life, I passed up an opportunity to panic Eve. I thought about what she said. It only made sense to follow the tracks, and there was no information to tell us which way the closest radio tower was, so we might as well go the direction the train went. "Good thinking," I said.

We walked along the tracks. Eve wandered back and forth between the dirt road beside the tracks and the tracks themselves. But I stayed on the tracks. My bare feet were cold and the wood across the tracks wasn't as cold as the sand.

Usually we're pretty strong hikers. We've gone all through the Poconos of Pennsylvania, and one summer we climbed around in the White Mountains of New Hampshire. But the blanket slowed Eve down a lot. It was way too big. I wished I had my knife so I could cut it the right length and she wouldn't have to drag it like that. I stopped her several times to fold the blanket in half, but somehow she always managed to get it all twisted and dragging within minutes.

"Look!" Eve pointed to the bulky thing up ahead. It wasn't moving and it made no noise.

I whispered, "I'll go first. Stay here." I walked ahead silent as a wombat. I didn't know if there were wombats in the desert, but I felt pretty sure they must be silent, since people said you were lucky if you ever spotted one anywhere. I stared. The bulky thing was a junked car, just as I'd suspected. I turned and called to Eve, "It's just . . ."

"I see." She was right behind me. So much for her short-lived obedience.

We both ran to the car. I don't know why, but somehow it reassured me. It was familiar.

But what lay about five feet off to the side of the car wasn't familiar at all. We went closer, walking slowly now. The wide, white teeth looked like the keys of a miniature piano. The hide was gone in most places, and a single tine of the rib cage stood up clean and white like a broken hoop. The body lay in three sections, though little parts of hide were scattered here and there. Only the tail seemed totally intact — a big, bushy horsetail. The shoes were still attached to the hooves. The most amazing thing of all was that there was no trace of wetness anywhere. The desert had sucked the corpse dry as powder.

Eve's breath beside me came loud and heavy. I didn't want her to start crying again. I took her by the hand and led her away.

"Do you think the car hit it?" she asked.

"Maybe. Or maybe a train hit it. Or maybe it just died of old age." That's what I hoped. I didn't want it to have died from some mysterious desert malady that would reach out and choke Eve and me. What was a horse doing out here anyway? It must have escaped from its owner and joined a wild herd. Did they have wild horse herds in Australia? They had wild camels, after all. "Yeah, old age killed it."

Eve shuddered. "Or maybe it got lost and died of that high thing."

"What high thing?"

"You know. What you said before. You said we were about to die of some high thing or get eaten by animals."

"Dehydration," I said. "It means drying out from lack of water. It has nothing to do with 'high.'"

"Oh."

"But it's not going to happen to us," I added quickly. "Trains come along here all the time. We'll flag one down long before we even get thirsty."

She nodded.

I swallowed and realized with alarm that I was thirsty already. It was the power of suggestion. It had to be. I stood beside the car and swallowed my own saliva over and over again.

"No tires," said Eve suddenly. She kicked at the right front door of the car, just like she'd kicked at the toilet seat in our train bathroom when she couldn't figure out how to get it down. Eve was an idiot kicker.

The door fell off, knocking Eve to the ground. A giant lizard looked right at us.

"A goanna," whispered Eve. She stood up slowly and walked backwards.

The goanna stood its ground on the ripped vinyl of the car's front seat. It must have been six feet long — maybe longer. It flicked its tongue. It puffed out its throat. It seemed almost like a dragon.

I looked around for a weapon. One of those cross wrenches to loosen and tighten tire lug nuts stuck out from under the rear of the car. I grabbed and pulled. The wrench came free and the right side of the car wobbled and clanked. The goanna slowly crawled through the missing front windshield and out onto the hood of the car. I could see the whole thing now. It was definitely more than six feet, and most of it was tail. Its claws made scratching noises on the rusty metal. It looked over its shoulder at us — just one eye, staring.

"Come on, Eve." I held out one hand to her and brandished the wrench with the other. I sort of remembered reading in the travel guide that goannas weren't generally dangerous. But what did "generally" mean? If this one was dangerous only once and the once was now, that was enough for me.

"Careful, Zach," whispered Eve. "Don't go near the horse."

"The horse? Are you nuts? The horse is dead."

"He belongs to the goanna."

This was crazy talk even for Eve. "What?"

"The goanna's a carrion eater. You know, he eats dead things."

"I know what *carrion* means," I snapped. After all, she wasn't the only one who read about animals. Still, it was clear she knew more about goannas than I did. I hadn't even recognized what it was at first. "Go on, tell me what you know," I said in a conciliatory tone.

"He'll protect his horse corpse from us."

"Even all dried out like that?"

"Maybe. He might like the hide."

"Oh." So the lizard was dangerous, after all. I had to keep it at bay. I lowered my chin and tried to look ferocious. I must have looked ridiculous.

The goanna waited, frozen like a rock. Our luck was still with us.

Eve took my hand again and we walked backwards to the train tracks, just a few feet away. The goanna crawled back into the front seat of the car, but it held its head up high and watched us.

"Run," I said.

"My blanket," said Eve.

I stared at her. She shivered in her short-sleeve shirt and ripped skirt. I looked back at the car. The blanket stuck out from under the fallen-off door. Our luck had just turned to mud. The goanna was still looking at us. Nothing was easy. But what choice did I have? It was already cold enough that I wished I had on more than my sweatsuit. Eve would be too cold to move at all if I didn't get the blanket back. I was cursed. But the goanna was a reptile — so it was cold blooded. It could probably hardly move at night. "Stay here," I said. I looked at her. "I mean it."

"Okay."

"Really."

"I said okay."

I half tiptoed back to the car. The goanna kept one eye on me. Then it flicked its head to the other side and stared with the other eye. I held the wrench ready with my right hand as I circled around the door. I tugged at the blanket with my left hand. The goanna jumped down out of the car, its front legs landing on the fallen-off door. I leaped backwards. It opened its jaws. I could see a row of sharp-pointed pearly teeth. The jaws closed with a hollow snapping sound — so much for slow-moving, cold-blooded reptiles. "All I want is the blanket," I said softly. I knew it was stupid to talk to a giant lizard, but the words just came. And as long as I talked, it kept me from picturing a short boy wrestling with a giant lizard in the cold desert.

The goanna snapped its jaws again. It had many small, sharp teeth. Many. It snapped a third time.

"You don't have a great personality, do you?" I whispered. Could we possibly do without the blanket? Was there any other way to keep Eve warm?

"Boom!" said Eve loudly. "Boom, boom, boom, boom!"

I looked at her in alarm.

"Boom!" She kept up a regular beat. For sure, she'd gone mad. She stood in the middle of the tracks booming with all her might.

I looked back at the goanna. It was looking at Eve.

"Boom!" shouted Eve. "Boom, boom, boom, boom!"

The goanna seemed baffled, if a goanna can be baffled. This was my chance. I stepped forward and grabbed a corner of the blanket again. The goanna kept its eyes on Eve, who boomed away like the bell of doom. I pulled gingerly. The blanket moved, along with the car door and the front half of the goanna. The goanna swung its head and looked at me.

"Boom!" hollered Eve, louder than ever.

The goanna looked back at her.

I held the wrench ready and pulled the blanket. The blanket and car door and goanna all moved, the goanna's front legs still perched on the door. I dragged the whole mess a few feet. The goanna's back legs waddled along steadily, but its face stayed fixed: its eye was intently on booming Eve. This wasn't ideal. I yanked. The blanket moved a little more out from under the door until the handle of the door caught on the material and stuck fast. The goanna blinked at me, than he turned back to Eve and her incessant boom. I gave the blanket the biggest jerk I could manage. It pulled free and I fell backwards. The goanna looked at me and flicked its tongue.

"Boom!" screamed Eve. "Boom, boom, boom!"

The goanna looked back at her. I picked up the blanket and walked backwards slowly. I realized that I was walking in time to Eve's booming. It was an eerie sensation. Then I had a sudden brainstorm. I dropped the blanket and ran to the car. I used the wrench to pry a section of chrome strip off the side, the whole time keeping my body tense and ready to swing the wrench at the goanna if it should attack. The goanna didn't even look at me. It stared right at Eve. I held the wrench and chrome strip in one hand and went over toward the goanna, just close enough to grab the blanket in the other hand. Then I walked backwards, quickly now, to Eve, letting her booming guide my steps. I stumbled over the blanket.

The goanna watched us. If it had any brains at all, I'm sure it was convinced we were insane. I was half convinced of it myself.

As soon as I reached Eve, she stopped booming. The silence startled me. Everything seemed immediately transformed — stark. We were lost in the middle of a never-ending desert with a giant goanna. Fear stabbed in my gut. We turned tail and ran along the tracks. When I looked back, the car was just a small bump in the distance and the goanna was nowhere in sight.

"Here." I stopped and handed Eve one end of the blanket. I controlled my breathing so that it came back to normal again. "You hold it tight."

She panted and her head hung forward. But she grabbed the blanket's edge with fingers that looked like claws in the moonlight. Adrenalin had done its job in both of us. Our eyes met and gradually I sensed her body relaxing. My own body felt like a formless lump of clay by now. My mouth was dry. I would have given anything — or almost anything — for a glass of water. Eve was doing something funny with her mouth. Swallowing, I thought. I mustn't mention thirst to her.

I focused on the job at hand. With the sharp chrome I opened a hole in the middle of the blanket. Then I pulled with both hands and managed to rip it pretty evenly down the center. I left Eve holding half the blanket and looking at me doubtfully. I would have been angry at that look just about any other time, but right now I was grateful to see her returning to her normal self. Plus, if she didn't trust me, maybe she wouldn't do what I said. And if she didn't do what I said, it wouldn't be my fault if she died.

She wouldn't die. I wouldn't die. We were going to be rescued any minute now.

Sure. By what? A flying saucer?

No use thinking that way. Keep focused.

I made a hole in the center of the half of the blanket that I was holding. Then I stuck it over Eve's head.

"Oh, a poncho!" She held out both arms. The poncho reached clear down to her ankles. Eve danced in a circle. She looked like a deformed, deranged bat.

I took the remaining half from Eve and made myself a second poncho. It came down to mid-calf, which was plenty for me, since I had sweat-pants on.

"You're so smart," Eve said, looking at me with admiration.

For the second time in one day she seemed almost nice. I took the risk. "Why'd you say, 'Boom'?"

"Chipmunks love rhythmic noises."

"Chipmunks?" I said weakly.

"Uh-huh. I read a book once about a girl who caught a chipmunk by banging a stick against a log. Rhythmic noises sort of hypnotize them."

I spoke carefully. "That was a goanna, not a chipmunk, remember?"

"Of course I remember. But I couldn't think of anything else. Anyway, it worked." Eve swatted at a fly. "I think we surprised him."

Against all reason, I found myself laughing.

Eve laughed, too.

When we stopped laughing, we walked silently

and quickly along the tracks. The moon was brighter than ever.

Eve grabbed my arm and pointed. I held up the wrench, ready for whatever it was. What I saw were two kangaroos bouncing along in the distance.

And once we passed a colony of bandicoots that had made a burrow in the embankment of the railroad. They had long, pointy snouts and big stick-up ears and rings on their tails. And they weren't shy at all. They watched us without budging. I'd have enjoyed them under any other circumstance. And Eve would have been delighted, I knew. But as it was, we just walked by them without pausing.

We walked for hours, swatting at flies. My eyes burned from staring into the distance, trying to make sure nothing snuck up on us. My neck hurt from holding it so tight and jerking it every which way. Each passing moment brought home how desolate this desert was, how desperate our situation was. We walked without pause, dry and silent. I don't know why Eve kept her silence. But I kept mine in order to hold the terror at bay.

I couldn't help looking at the sky. It was all around us, coming clear down to the sand as though we were in a giant planetarium. The Milky Way stood out sharply and the constellations were brighter than I'd ever seen them before. This was not the same sky I knew at home. Nothing was in its familiar place. I thought of sailors who guided their ships by the stars in the old days. Here in the southern hemisphere the stars wouldn't help me at all. We were as lost as anyone ever had been.

I'm not the world's best at estimating time without a watch. But I'm sure we walked for at least three hours before we saw it. I couldn't believe it at first, so I didn't say anything to Eve. I didn't want to get her hopes up. I thought it might be my version of a mirage — instead of an oasis. But I walked faster. And sure enough, it was true: a radio tower loomed in the night. We ran, stumbling like drunkards. But it wasn't the same as the towers I'd seen from the train. This one didn't have a satellite dish on top. It had solar panels. What lousy luck. My head felt heavy and my feet were like ice stumps and I needed this to be an ordinary radio tower, with all the stuff that radio towers were supposed to have, not some stupid solar power something or other. Still, there was a little cement house beside the radio tower. It had to have a person inside. It just had to.

Chapter 6

The Radio

The padlock on the door of the cement house was clean and new and there was no doorbell. I didn't bother knocking. If anyone was inside, that person was locked in and dead by now. Nope, the cement house was empty. But it still had to have something important inside. And I was determined to get in there. "You wouldn't think they'd be so tough on security out here," I muttered angrily. I was half incoherent from lack of sleep. It was the middle of the night already. "It isn't like there are hordes of people around to keep out."

Eve looked at the padlock. "They're keen on maintenance, I guess." Her voice was completely normal — without a trace of weariness.

"Keen!" I shouted. "Do you have to talk that phony Australian talk all the time?"

"We're in Australia," said Eve with composure.

"We're also in a desperate situation. Act right."

"What do you want me to do, shout like you?" Eve threw her head back. "Ahhhhhhh!"

I stared at her. Then I threw my head back, too. "Ahhhhhhh!" I screamed.

When she stopped, I stopped. We looked at each other, but I think we were both too tired to do anything more. I raised the wrench and banged away at the padlock. The lock dented easily, but it didn't give way. It got flatter and flatter. I banged relentlessly, swinging with all my might. The lock was flat and dented and still functional. I dropped to the sandy dirt that no longer looked red, but only gray in the moonlight, and covered my face with my hands. Exhaustion swept over me. Sweat rolled down my back. I thought about how unfair that was, given that my toes were frozen stiff.

Eve patted my shoulder, like she'd patted my back when I vomited. She picked up the wrench and gave one whammo whack to the padlock.

The wrench flew out of her hands and landed with a dull whump in the sand. She sank down beside me, silent.

I waited for some wise-guy remark from her about how I should be opening the door, not sitting on the ground. Instead she kept silent. Nothing seemed to move anywhere. The flies were long gone.

"Go on," said Eve finally. "Say it."

"Huh?" I said.

"Say it. Say I can't even keep that yucky whatever it is — tool thing — in my hands. Just like I can't catch a ball. And I can't keep my balance."

"What are you talking about?"

"Like when you saw me trip at my ballet recital." Eve punched me in the shoulder. "Go ahead. Say I never do anything right. Say I'm stupid. Pinch me, you big old blob."

"I don't want to pinch you."

"Why not? You kept pinching me on the train."

"You kept saying things to get us in trouble."

"See? I knew you were thinking that. Go ahead. Say it. Say all those mean, ugly, nasty, mean things you always say." Eve threw herself backwards and lay flat on the sand. "I'll just look at the stars till I become one." Her voice was quiet and lonely. "Then you'll be sorry."

I looked at the stars. Blazing balls of fire, zillions of miles away. From here they looked cold as diamonds. I looked down at Eve beside me, stretched out full length like that. If she were dead, her coffin would be short. "I didn't see you trip at your recital." I rubbed my throat and swallowed the dry, hard lump. My eyes were dry now, too. And my skin felt parched. "You know what they say about performers: if you mess up and keep going, that's almost better than if you did it perfect in the first place."

Eve didn't answer.

I got up and walked over to the wrench. This was our best chance. I had to smash that lock till my body couldn't move anymore. I positioned myself as if I were at bat and swung with all my might. I half expected to hear, "Strike one." Instead, I heard a clunk as the lock fell on the little ledge of cement that surrounded the cement house.

Eve sat up. She seemed dazed for a moment. Then she came over next to me. We opened the door together. The room was dark inside. I felt along the wall for a switch. Something crawled onto my hand. I flicked it off and shuddered.

Eve saw. "Why did you jerk your hand?"

I didn't answer. I wouldn't think about poisonous spiders. We needed a light. I felt the wall again. This time I hit the switch. The room lit up from a single bare bulb overhead. Beside the switch was a rack of automobile-like batteries. They must have held the solar panels' power overnight and on overcast days.

The space was about the size of a walk-in closet. It was bare, except for a desk-like shelf that hung from one wall with a long switchboard on it that had four meters set in it. Mounted above the shelf was a big metal box. One section of the metal box was a grid of punched holes that had to be a small loudspeaker. Along the lower edge of the box was a knob and then a series of toggle switches. There were labels above each switch. I leaned forward to read them: FS1. RSX. Things like that. Undecipherable abbreviations. Hanging on a hook at the side of the metal box was an ordinary little microphone.

I picked up the mike and turned the knob-dial

all the way to the right. Nothing happened. Several points were labeled around the dial. So I turned it very slowly all the way to the left, stopping at each labeled point. Not a whisper of static from the loudspeaker. Nothing.

I figured the switches on the board had to do with controlling the amplifier and the dial had to do with finding channels. But one of the toggles on the metal box or on the switchboard also had to be the on-off for the whole unit. I threw a switch and fiddled with the dial and threw another switch and fiddled some more. Nothing. I threw switches wildly.

Eve caught my panic. She banged at the switches on the board.

I grabbed her hands and held them tight. "It's okay. All we have to do is find the right switch. Breaking it won't help."

Eve nodded. She was clearly working hard to control herself. "I'll start at one end?"

"Yeah, sure." I held the mike in one hand and turned the dial to each labeled point, left and right, as Eve threw switches, mechanically covering every switch on the board and every toggle on the metal box. "Maybe it takes a combination of switches." I pushed the left-most switch and left it on. Then Eve and I began again, her throwing switches and me turning the dial, one switch after another. Then I went to the next switch. And on and on.

Static came through the loudspeaker.

"Stop," I shouted at Eve, just as her hand moved to the next switch. "That's it. Okay." The loudspeaker was now receiving. "Hello," I said into the mike. "Hello!" There was no answer. Probably no one had heard me. How could I send a message? I was afraid to touch the switches for fear that if the whole thing turned off again, it would take forever to re-create the combination that had made it alive. We'd have to start all over. Still, I had to figure out how to send a message. I clutched the mike desperately.

"Look." Eve put her face close to the mike. She reached out and pressed a button on its side. "Hello," she said into the mike. "Hello."

There was no response. But now I remembered a movie I'd seen with truck drivers who talked to each other on shortwave radios. You pressed the button to send, and released it to receive. "Let go of the button."

Eve took her hand away.

"Hello, hello," came a voice through the loud-speaker. Then there was a click.

"Help!" I shouted.

"Hello," came the voice. "Hello, hello. Who's there?" *Click.*

How stupid could I be? I pressed the button. "Help!" I shouted again.

"Help, help!" shouted Eve, looking at me with crazed eyes.

I put my finger against my lips in the hush signal to Eve. Then I took a deep breath. I tried to speak normally. "Help. We're lost at a radio tower." I released the button.

"Who are you?" *Click.*

Press. "It's me and my sister. We're Americans." Release.

"I can hear that. Where are your parents?" *Click.*

Pressing the button came automatically now. "We were on the Ghan alone. We got thrown off the train."

"You what?" *Click.*

By now I pressed the button the instant I

heard his click. "We got . . ." Oh, it didn't matter. "Please come get us."

"On the Ghan, you say?"

"We're lost!"

"Certainly. Yes."

"We can't walk anymore."

"You're hurt?"

"No. We're tired and cold and lost. We can't walk one step more."

"It wouldn't be advisable, no." The voice seemed to think awhile — static and background noise came from the loudspeaker. "Which radio tower are you at?"

At least I could answer that one without hesitation. "The one with the solar panels on top instead of the satellite dish."

The man snorted. I was pretty sure he was muffling a laugh. "Lots of radio towers have solar panels. Which one are you at precisely?"

I didn't remember seeing a name anywhere. "I don't know. Where would the name be?"

"Go outside and read the mileage peg."

"What's a mileage peg?"

"It's a marker on the track for every kilometer.

We still call them mileage pegs, even though we switched over to the metric system years ago." He chuckled openly now. I didn't feel much like chuckling, given the situation, and I didn't like him for doing that. "Go on," he said. "Go outside and read the mileage peg."

"Okay. Hold on," I said. "Don't go away, please."

"I'm here, son."

I felt a little better with that. Maybe he wasn't such a bad guy, after all. I handed Eve the mike. "Keep him with us. Talk to him. I'll go look for the peg."

Eve nodded. She pressed the button. "Hello?"

I could imagine Eve driving the man on the radio nuts. But I decided not to tell her to shut up. Maybe if the man realized how crazy Eve was, he'd take our plight more seriously. I went outside and walked along the track till I found a peg with a number. 1152. That was easy enough to remember. I just hoped that was a mileage peg. I ran back to the cement house.

"A giant goanna," said Eve into the phone. "It had its own horse." She was half in tears.

I took the mike from her. "It's 1152."

"1152? Are you sure?"

"Yes." I clenched my teeth. If that wasn't a mileage peg, what was it?

"What time did you, ummm, did you descend, shall we say, from the Ghan?"

I remembered looking at my watch before I took it off when I got undressed for bed. We'd been thrown off within a half hour after that. "It must have been close to nine," I said.

"Nine P.M.," said the voice. "Well, that's about right. A little more than a quarter of the way. All right." He was silent. Then he clicked off.

"All right, what?" I said, working to keep from shouting.

"I'll be there to get you in . . ." he made a humming noise, "about twenty-two minutes."

"Really?" I wanted to dance and shout. "Who are you?"

"Frederick. And you?"

I laughed weakly. "I didn't mean what's your name. I'm Zach and my sister's Eve. But who are you? Are you coming in a police car or what?"

"Ah, you'll see. Just stay inside the pillbox and I'll be there. You'll hear me coming." He clicked off.

I put the mike down and looked at Eve.

She wiped a tear from her cheek.

"We're standing in a pillbox," I said.

Eve didn't even look at me. She was rubbing hard at her eyes.

"A pillbox. That's what they call these cement houses. As if we were little vitamin pills or something." That ought to cheer her up.

Eve made a small sob.

"Don't worry," I said. "He's coming for us."

"I'm not worried." She looked at me and her eyes shown bright as the moon. "I'm mad. He doesn't believe us."

"I'm not surprised."

"He wouldn't even let me talk. I tried to tell him he had to stop the men in the Ghan, but he told me to calm down and just describe everything that had happened since we'd been thrown off the train. Like I was hysterical or something." She stamped her foot. "He treated me like a stupid little kid. Like a liar."

I looked at her sad face. "Listen, we're going to be rescued. Eve, that's wonderful. Don't you see? We really could have . . ." She looked at me.

I couldn't say it. ". . . been in trouble," I ended lamely.

"I know." She pressed her lips together and hung her head. "It's just that they're bad men and they could have killed us and they're going to do something bad with that bird and they're going to get away with all of it unless someone does something about it right now!" She looked back up at me again and her eyes had a touch of accusation in them.

I felt like I'd been slugged. "It's not my fault! What can I do? What could anybody do about it right now?" Eve was being irrational. Like Mom always said, when Eve got overtired, she got irrational.

"Maybe he'd believe you. You're older. Everyone believes you. Take the mike and tell him to stop the men on the Ghan."

She was right. I could at least try. I pressed the button. "Hello, again?" I released it.

"Ahhh!" Eve jumped backwards and slammed against me. I fell across the switchboard. She pushed us both against the wall and pointed.

It came running at us, like a tiny lobster, claws

up and tail curled over its back, pointing right at her.

Eve screamed again.

My feet were bare. I leaned down and grabbed Eve's ankle and lifted it, as though she were a puppet. She grasped my back fast to keep from falling. I stomped her shoe down on the scorpion.

"Oh." Eve panted. "Oh, it could have killed us."

"Maybe. Yeah, maybe."

"Oh. I should have stepped on it myself." She hugged me tight. "I just didn't think right."

"It's okay." I enclosed her in both arms for a few minutes. Then I let go and looked around the room, carefully inspecting the corners of both floor and walls. I should have checked it all when we first came in. There was nothing. Had it been the scorpion that I'd felt crawl across my hand when I reached for the light switch? The hairs on my neck stood up.

"Yucky thing." Eve scraped her shoe on the cement floor. "Oh, no." She pointed at the loud-speaker. "It's dead again. The switches got pushed all crazy when I knocked into you."

I went over to the shelf and stared at the switchboard and the metal box above it. "What a stupid system. Whoever set this up thought that everyone who needed to use it would know what the abbreviations stood for. It's ridiculous. The whole thing should always be set for use." I blew air between my lips in frustration. Then I looked at Eve's face, all squinched with worry, and I knew I had to calm her down. "It doesn't matter, really. The man said he'd be here soon. We can have him radio ahead as soon as he picks us up."

Eve moved close beside me. "How long did he say?"

"Twenty minutes. And five have passed already. So he'll be here in fifteen minutes. That's hardly anything. What do you want to do in the meantime?"

"I want to stop those bad men. Let's figure out the radio combination again."

Her persistence made me mad. "I don't want to."

"Why not?"

I sighed. "I'm tired, Eve. Anyway, we have a better chance of convincing this guy in person.

Just wait." My voice was as firm as I could make it. "Forget it. I mean it."

"I could figure it out myself."

"I won't speak on the radio if you do."

She raised her arms out to both sides and for a second I had an image of her taking off into the night like a real bat. She might hate Beaky, but they had something in common — airborne, they might both be in their element. Eve dropped her arms in resignation. "I'm tired, too. I wish there was a bed."

"I know," I said softly. There was no point in being mad at her. Plus, I didn't have the energy. "Let's go outside and watch for the nocturnal animals of the desert."

"You sound like me," said Eve.

"I was trying to get your attention."

Eve shook her head. "You shouldn't go outside with bare feet. Not after the scorpion."

She was right again. I put my arm around her and we sat down side by side and waited. I rubbed my cold feet with my free hand. I yawned. It would be easy to fall asleep. Just close my eyes and let it happen. But I had to stay awake to listen for the guy who was coming.

What was his name? Fred. I had to make sure he found us. I stared out the door of the pillbox and concentrated on listening.

"Zach, it's not true that making a mistake and keeping on going is almost better than doing it perfect."

"Who says?"

"It isn't. But thanks for saying it."

"No sweat."

The floor beneath my bottom was hard and cold. If I weren't so tired, I'd shift around to try to get comfortable. But there'd be no point to that anyway — I had a skinny butt, no matter how I moved it.

"Zach?"

"What?"

"Do you think I'll look like Mom?"

"You already do."

"But do you think I'll be shaped like her? You know, when I'm a woman?"

I didn't want to think about it. Eve certainly had a knack for finding just the right thing to talk about in any given situation. I took my arm away from around her. "Talk to Mom about it."

"I don't want to talk to Mom. Mom always

says things will turn out fine. Mom's always cheerful."

"You're always cheerful."

"No I'm not."

"Yes you are."

"Am not."

"This is a stupid argument."

Eve wriggled around inside her poncho. She sighed. "Zach?"

"Hmmm?"

"Do you look like Dad?"

I closed my eyes and thought of Dad. I remembered his thick hair. And glasses. And he was big, with a soft belly. But I couldn't picture his face. I opened my eyes. "You've seen his photos."

"Photos aren't anything like people." Eve pulled at the tips of her hair. "You're so lucky."

"What do you mean?"

"You knew him."

"You knew him, too."

"I don't remember anything." Eve dropped her hands to the floor. "When Mom tells me about things he did, I try to remember. Sometimes I think I remember. But I don't really." Eve's hand came out from under her poncho and she rubbed her nose. "Sometimes I don't believe I ever had a father. It's like you and Mom made him up."

I nodded my head slowly. Eve was three when Dad died. Could I remember being three? "You've got Mom," I said gently.

"Yeah. She treats me like a baby."

I couldn't have agreed more. "You act like a baby." As soon as the words were out of my mouth, I regretted them.

"Are you going to be mean again?"

"Sorry. Habit, I guess."

"Sure." Eve's voice was sarcastic.

"I'm sorry. Really."

Eve looked at me, her face all earnest and unhappy. "Okay. Anyway, I don't act like a baby. I can't help the way she treats me."

I picked at the little nubby balls on my poncho. "She thinks everything you do is great."

Eve took my hand. "She's nice to you, too."

I gave a little laugh. "Not like she is to you."

"She loves you, just the same."

I knew Mom loved me. And I knew Eve couldn't help the way Mom treated her. Probably Mom couldn't even help the way she treated her. I looked at the ring on Eve's finger. "What's green mean?"

"What?"

I tapped her mood ring. "It's green now."

"Hope. That's right, too. A little while ago I thought maybe we'd die tonight. I thought I'd never get to be a woman, and, well, you know, do all those things women do. But now I'm hopeful. It's a good ring."

Hope. I was hopeful, too. "I can't remember him all the time, either. Dad, I mean."

"Really?"

"He used to carry you a lot. In his arms. Sometimes he'd carry you in one arm and me in the other."

"Oh."

"And he wore this hat in the car. You used to grab it and put it on. All the time."

"A hat . . ." Eve spoke slowly. "Like a baseball hat, only soft."

"That's right. Leather."

"Dark."

"Brown."

"I remember it." Eve smiled at me. "I can't remember him, but I remember the hat."

"Yeah? I still have it. I have a box of his things that Mom let me keep."

"Oh."

My stomach tightened. I never should have mentioned the box. I liked that hat. I hadn't opened the box for maybe a year, but I still liked that hat. Now Eve was going to ask me for it. I looked at her. She wasn't looking at me anymore. She was sort of looking vaguely out the pillbox door, with that smile still on her face. I had a big silver ring of keys that had been Dad's, too. He used to let me hold them. They didn't fit in my pocket. They were heavy and wonderful. And I had a pencil of his that had letters on the side. They said, "Speak of the devil." Dad was an anthropologist, too, like Mom. He studied different peoples' ideas of devils. And he loved that pencil. He didn't use it — he just kept it in a cup on his desk. And I had one of his baby teeth. Grandma gave me that. Grandma is very crazy. Sort of like Eve. When Eve asked for the hat, which she was bound to do within the next three seconds, I'd offer her the tooth, instead. She'd love it. Or I'd get her to love it. I'd make her feel it was special. Eve always wanted anything that I said was great. And I wouldn't care if I had to give up the tooth, because I was afraid to touch it anyway. I was afraid it would fall apart.

Eve took a loud breath. This was it. I had to make the tooth sound wonderful. But no. She didn't look at me. She didn't talk. She just twirled the ring around and around on her finger. I watched it slowly change colors. It went from green to purple.

CHAPTER 7

Tarcoola

Eve heard the rumble before me. It started out like a low whine. She squeezed my hand. The whine got louder. I rose with difficulty and walked stiff-legged out of the pillbox. I had to concentrate to keep from shivering. I picked up the wrench without thinking and walked to the tracks. "Yes! It's a train."

We stood on the ties and looked toward the north, toward Alice Springs. I couldn't figure out how a train could cover all that distance in twenty-two minutes. Then I realized how stupid my thought was. Of course, the train had already been on the track when my message got through. That was why there was so much background noise on the radio when the guy was talking.

Exhaustion had made me dopey. What did it matter, anyway? The train was in sight now, and what a glorious sight it was.

Eve jumped up and down beside me.

I jumped, too. Then I stopped fast. My bare feet, to which feeling had not returned, were tender from the long walk on the rough wood ties of the tracks. I waved both arms over my head. The poncho blanket flapped around me. The train whistle split the cold night air like an arrow splashing into still water. The brakes screeched.

We stood to one side of the tracks and waited as the marvelous freight train came to a halt.

A man leaned out the side window at the front of the locomotive. "Zach and Eve? I told you you'd hear me coming." He laughed.

"Fred?" I called.

"Frederick. That's me." He waved his hat. Then he disappeared. We waited. And as we waited, I examined the locomotive. It had a squared-off cowcatcher out front and windows that wrapped around to doors on both sides. Back from the door on our side was a ladder that went up the side of the train to the roof. And back from that was a door that went into a rear, windowless section of the locomotive. It was huge. The cargo cars that followed were open to the sky, but I couldn't tell what was in them. There were a lot of them — dozens, for sure.

I had finished my inspection and we were still waiting. Surely three or four minutes had passed. How long could it take Frederick just to get out of the train? When I was about to shout, he reappeared around the front. He stuck out his lips as though he was thinking hard. "Well, you look pretty good, considering."

"Thanks," said Eve. She swayed and I thought she would fall. Frederick caught her before I could.

"What time is it?" I asked, not quite sure why I cared.

Frederick smiled at me. "Very late. Come on, climb up into the train." We went up into the front of the train. There was only one seat and Frederick took it. "Make yourselves at home on the floor. It's the best I can offer. We don't carry passengers, generally."

"Just like goannas don't attack, generally," I said.

"What's that?"

"Nothing."

Frederick frowned at me. "Wait here just one minute." He got off the train and I watched him through the window as he turned off the light in the pillbox and closed the door. He inspected the broken lock, then pocketed it and came back into the train. "Did you use that wrench to bust the lock?"

I realized I was still holding the wrench. I hugged it, though I wasn't afraid. Frederick looked and acted like a decent sort. "Yes."

"Mighty lucky you had a wrench on you."

"We found it by an old junked car."

Frederick nodded. "I guess that's it, then." He started up the train and we gained speed fast.

"I'm thirsty," said Eve. "And hungry, too."

"Sorry about that," said Frederick. "I'm all out of tucker. But you can drink from my water bottle here, and I'll get you something better at the first stop." He pointed to a plastic bottle on the floor by his foot.

Eve took the bottle and drank. She handed it to me. I drank greedily. It was the most delicious water I'd ever tasted in my life.

"Talk on the radio now, Zach," said Eve into my ear. "Call the Ghan."

"Okay, leave it to me."

Eve nodded. She gave me a silly smile. Then she curled up on the floor and fell instantly asleep.

I put the water bottle back by Frederick's foot and stood there blinking, forcing my eyes to stay open. We were going fast. Very fast. "What time is it?" And this time, I knew why I was asking.

"Ah, yes." Frederick held his watch up for me to see. I tried to focus on it. He laughed. "You're a tired young man. It's four minutes after one in the morning. What do you think of that? You ever been up this late before?"

I shook my head. "How fast can you go?"

"Well, now, let's see. Generally I average about ninety, ninety-five kilometers an hour."

"And the Ghan? How fast does it go?"

"Oh, the Ghan can manage eighty, tops. Of course, the Ghan makes more stops than I do, so that slows her down a lot, too."

"What's your top speed?"

"Well, I don't really know what she can do. A lot faster than ninety-five, I'm sure. Freight trains go slow so the tracks don't wear out too soon."

"How fast, Frederick?"

"Well, you've got to be careful, because if you go too fast, she can jump the tracks. Plus, we're pulling forty loads of copper from Tennant Creek, so braking time is increased and you're in trouble if you can't brake fast because of all the animal herds that cross the tracks."

"How fast is too fast?"

Frederick pointed. "See this dial here. When the rpm's get over to around here . . ." He tapped his finger. "That's when you're in danger." He looked ahead into the night.

I moved closer to him. "What's the very fastest we could do?"

He looked at me slyly. "You want to catch up with the Ghan, that it?"

"Yes."

Frederick chuckled. "I've already thought about that. Right now if I went faster, by the time I saw something on the tracks, it would be too late to stop. But as soon as dawn comes and I have a good long view of the tracks, I'll speed it up enough to intercept the Ghan at Port

Augusta. That's the Ghan's last stop before Adelaide. It'll only give you an hour on the train before the end of the line, but an hour is an hour." He sounded proud. "That way your aunt won't be worried about you."

My heart did a little skip. "How'd you know my aunt was coming to meet us?"

"I talked with your porter."

"You talked to Eugene?"

"Eugene. That's right." He smiled. "Twice. The conductor on the Ghan heard our exchange."

"How?"

Frederick looked at me and laughed. "It's not like a private telephone, you know. The radio waves are open to everyone. I hear anything that's said and everyone else hears anything I say."

"Well, what did Eugene say?"

"The instant the engineer told him that two American kids were lost in the desert, he checked your compartment. When it was empty, he made an announcement over the train's intercom, asking if anyone had seen you two."

I remembered the little speaker that came on

when Eve and I were in Beaky's compartment, telling about the camel herd. So now Beaky and No Brains knew we'd been found.

Frederick leaned back in his seat. "No one had, so he came on the radio and talked to me — asked me your names again, because the engineer couldn't remember what you'd said. Eve and Zach, that's what I told him. And he said you belonged on the Ghan all right. That part of your story is true." He shook his head. "You got Eugene pretty upset."

"Can you get a message through to Eugene now?"

"You mean to let him know you're fine? I already did that when I stopped the train just now. Had to let him know before he went back to bed. Otherwise I doubt he would have slept a wink. He went off happy as could be, prepared to announce the good news to the whole train. Some of them were worried about you, of course. Now they all know you'll be catching up at Port Augusta."

I shook my head. Beaky and No Brains knew we had been picked up. They knew we would reboard the train at Port Augusta. That gave them plenty of time to conceal the bird. "Could you send Eugene another message?"

"Another?" Frederick scratched the back of his neck. "Why don't you just curl up like your sister and sleep awhile? We can talk about it when you wake up."

"This is important." The train jerked and I almost fell. I braced myself against the instrument console to the left of Frederick's chair. "We need to tell Eugene about a crime."

Frederick pursed his lips. "A crime?"

"We were thrown from the train."

Frederick scratched the back of his neck again. He kept his eyes on the tracks ahead. "The train slowed down almost to a stop because of a camel herd — Eugene told me all about it. Children love to see camels. Especially American children. You don't have them at home. It's understandable."

My heart beat hard as his words sank in. "You think we got off by ourselves."

"You should have known better. It might have ended very differently, it might. It was dangerous.

135

But there's no point in lying to cover it up. Nobody's angry. Children have bad judgment. Everybody knows that."

"I'm thirteen," I said loudly, but my voice wasn't too impressive; I was so tired, I was slurring my words. I licked my lips and spoke as slowly and clearly as I could. "Thirteen-year-olds know enough not to get off a train in the middle of the desert."

"Some thirteen-year-olds might not be too sensible."

"Do I look like I'm not sensible?"

Frederick stole a quick glance at me. I tried to look alert and sensible, but I knew I wasn't doing a good job at it. My mouth felt like dirty cotton and my eyes were on fire. Frederick didn't look happy. A light mounted on top of the instrument console came on right then. Frederick quickly reached for a little lever beside the light and turned it ninety degrees. The light went off.

"What was that?"

"It's insurance, in a way. I'll tell you about it in the morning. For now, go to sleep, son."

Yes, I thought, all I wanted was to sleep. "The men in the compartment next to ours, the last compartment in our train carriage, they had a bird that's illegal to own."

Frederick didn't say a word.

The rhythm of the train was rocking me to sleep. I forced myself to keep talking. "When we discovered the bird, they threw us off the train to keep us from telling about it."

Frederick shook his head. "Animals aren't allowed in the compartments."

"They snuck it on." The train lurched and my head shook so hard, I thought it would fall off.

"Your porter, that Eugene, saw their birdcage. I asked him about it. You see, your sister told a rather . . . unusual story." Frederick looked at me anxiously. He clearly thought Eve had lost her marbles. And it looked like he wondered if I had, too. I tried to look sane. He turned his eyes back to the track ahead. "They're stuffed crows. For their act." He glanced over and gave me a quick, small smile, and I could see he felt sorry for me. "They're clowns. Probably pretty good ones. They fooled you. Children get fooled easily by clowns."

"They had stuffed birds in the cage when they got on, but a real bird was inside a stocking."

"A stocking?"

"A woman's stocking." I was aware of how absurd my words sounded. I tried to look sincere. Frederick had to believe me.

"You saw a bird in a stocking?" His voice had turned worried.

"No. I saw an empty stocking with a feather and bird droppings in it." That sounded truly awful. "But I saw the bird. Eve and I both saw it. It's as real as you and I are." Though right then I wasn't sure how real I was.

Frederick rubbed his hand across his mouth and stared out at the tracks ahead. "A lie like this would be grave, son. I tell you, you're not in trouble for getting off the train."

"I'm not lying." My head was banging by now. I wanted to fall on the floor and just sleep forever.

Frederick glanced quickly at me again. "I wonder . . . Tell me a bit more."

"It was a cockatoo."

"Americans generally don't know much about birds."

"My sister knows every bird in Australia. She'll tell you we saw a cockatoo. Ask her."

Frederick's eyes turned to Eve. I looked, too. She was on her back with her mouth open and she looked as good as dead. "It'll have to wait," he said softly.

"Couldn't you just radio the Ghan and tell them to check the birdcage again? Please, Frederick. Please."

"Look, Eugene's asleep now. If we wake him for a lot of nonsense, he won't like either of us much."

"It's not nonsense."

Frederick made a clicking noise with his tongue. "Don't give up, do you? Well, you can radio them at dawn. How's that?"

"But we can't let the men get away."

"There's nowhere for them to go, son. It's got to wait."

Wait. Everything would have to wait. Everything could wait. Couldn't it? Eve said the men would get away with it. She had looked at me with accusation. But it had to wait. It wasn't my fault. My eyes kept closing. "Black cockatoo," I insisted, or I thought I insisted. I wasn't sure what I said. Whatever I said, it had to wait.

"Tell you what. I'll go as fast as I can safely go

all night long — to make absolutely sure we catch the Ghan at Port Augusta."

"Top speed to Port Augusta," I said. "Go, Frederick."

"That's right. Now give it a rest, son."

I could barely hear the words. I shut my eyes and dropped.

Slam! I woke as my face smashed against the inner wall of the locomotive. The train had stopped. I turned over just in time to see Frederick climb down out the side door.

Eve cried out from the corner where she had curled up when we first got on the train. "Ouch. I bit my tongue."

"Too bad." I crawled over beside her.

"Why'd we stop? Are we there?"

"I don't know." I got up and looked out the window. It was still nighttime. We were at a tiny station. The sign read, "Tarcoola." In the station lights I could see two men feeding a huge hose into the side of the train. "We're refueling," I said to Eve.

She stood up beside me. "It's still dark out."

I strained to make out the time on the big station clock, but the angle was wrong and I couldn't see it.

Eve walked to the front of the locomotive and ran her hand along the back of the driver's seat. Then she turned to me with excitement in her voice. "We could do it, Zach. We could drive the train on our own and catch up with the Ghan and . . ."

"Don't be crazy. We have to think things over. We're not even fully awake yet." I pulled her away from the driver's seat. I was stunned at her crazy idea, even if I'd had some vague form of that very idea myself. But at the same time it thrilled me to hear it said out loud like that. "We'll do something, I promise. But we have to figure out what. Come on." I went back to the window.

Frederick stood on the loading platform and talked with another man dressed in the same train uniform. The man held a small picnic cooler. I felt instantly hungry. A third man came out of the station building and walked up to the man who was talking to Frederick. He went back into the station. Then he returned with a couple of plastic containers of what looked like water. I felt instantly thirsty.

Eve walked toward the door of the train.

I was beside her in a flash. "Where're you going?"

"I have to pee."

Now that she mentioned it, I wouldn't mind finding a bathroom myself. Plus, a bathroom would have a sink with drinking water. "Let's go."

We climbed off the train. Eve tripped over her blanket poncho and fell off the bottom step, landing splat on the wooden platform.

Frederick looked at us. "What're you two up to?" He sounded edgy. Or maybe annoyed. The last thing we needed was for Frederick to be annoyed with us. We needed his cooperation.

"Bathroom," I said, helping Eve to her feet. I gave a sheepish smile.

The man holding the cooler smiled back. It was a big friendly cockeyed smile. He pointed. "That way." Then all three men walked off through the center door of the station building. I could read the station clock now: four-thirty.

How far had we come? I couldn't afford to sleep anymore. As soon as we got started, I had to get Frederick to make that radio call. I hurried for the bathroom. Eve followed.

There was only one bathroom for men and women — way around the side. And from the looks of the decor inside I was pretty sure not too many women had ever been in it. A magazine lay on the floor. I could tell from the cover it was the kind with pictures of naked women in it. And that was about the brightest thing in the place. But at least the toilet was separated from the sink and urinal area by a partition wall that went halfway across the room.

I pulled the door shut behind us. There was no lock button on the knob and no hook to close it securely. I didn't like that. Privacy in the bathroom is something I count on. I opened the door a little way and peeked outside. No one else seemed to be coming. Probably no one would interrupt us. I shut the door hard.

I let Eve go first. While I was waiting for her, I splashed my face in the sink water and drank several handfuls.

Eve finished and I took my turn fast.

Then I went to open the door. It wouldn't open. I twisted on the knob. It turned, but the door wouldn't open. I pushed hard. There was no doubt about it: the door was jammed. I bashed on the door with all my weight. I bashed and bashed. Eve bashed away beside me.

I stopped. "It's no use, Eve."

But she was already screaming: "Help! Get us out of here! Help!"

Her voice was deafening in the tiny bathroom, but I was pretty sure no one outside could hear us — unless someone had locked us in! The idea jolted me. "Shhh, Eve. Be quiet. Let me think."

Eve shut up just like that. She stood beside me, working to catch her breath from the bashing and screaming, her eyes glued to me.

"Someone might have locked us in," I said in the calmest voice I could muster.

Eve nodded and kept looking at me.

I chewed on my bottom lip. I should have carried the wrench in with me. Then I could have knocked a hole through the door. I looked around, then up. Yes. There was a circular slatted cover

over a vent in the ceiling. "Maybe we can take off the cover and climb out."

"You're not tall enough," said Eve.

"You are, if you stand on my shoulders."

Eve looked at me with huge eyes. "I'll fall."

"Okay, you're right." I climbed up onto the sink. "Hold my legs to keep me steady."

Eve hugged me around the legs. I thought she was going to make me fall, she hugged so tight. But I didn't say anything. It felt good to have her close.

I stood up slowly. I had to hunch over so my head wouldn't hit the ceiling. Then I reached for the vent cover. It was too far away from the sink. I climbed down. "Listen, Eve, I'll stand right under the vent cover. If you climb onto the sink, you can step from there onto my shoulders, and you'll be able to push against the ceiling to steady yourself."

"Why don't you do it?"

"I can't stand on your shoulders, Eve. I'd kill you."

"What if I can't get the cover off?"

"Try."

"What if I get out and someone's waiting for me? Someone awful?"

I looked at her face. She looked so much like Mom right now, I wanted to cry. "You're right, Eve. We can stay here till someone finds us."

"Then those bad men will get away with the bird." Eve opened and shut her hands fast, as though she was grasping for something. I thought for a moment she was going to flip out on me. But then she climbed onto the sink. I held my arms out stiffly so that even from where I stood, I could steady her a bit. She pushed both hands against the ceiling and put one foot on my shoulder. Then she sort of leaped and put the other foot on my other shoulder. I wobbled. She was heavier than I expected. I couldn't keep this up for long. And I just knew she'd never figure out how to take off the vent cover.

In an instant the cover clattered to the floor. "It wasn't even attached with screws," said Eve. "It was just sort of wedged up here."

"Well, can you climb out?"

"I've got my head out, and my shoulders. I don't see anyone hanging around."

I felt her lift away from me. Her legs kicked

out. I put my hands under her feet and pushed her upwards. She disappeared through the hole in the ceiling.

I heard a scrambling on the roof, then a clunk outside the door. "Ouch." And, finally, "Oh." The door opened.

I took Eve by the hand and ran, expecting every second to be grabbed from behind. We went around to the front of the station and inside. We made it.

The station was empty except for a man who lay on a cot behind a counter. "Mister, wake up," I said. "Please wake up."

The man sat up. He smiled a bit groggily. "I'm not asleep, laddie. What can I do for you?"

"We're in trouble. You have to help us."

He stood up and came over. "Tell me about it."

"Someone's after us. He locked us in the bathroom."

"The bathroom here at the station, you mean?"

"Yes. Just now."

The man laughed. "Did you slam the door?"

"What?" Was he crazy?

"Slam it? Did you slam it, when you closed it?"

"No. I shut it firmly."

"That's all it takes. The little latch outside just flops around on the rickety frame. People who don't know about it are getting shut in there all the time. It's a bit of a giggle, it is."

"Oh." My cheeks went hot. Was that really all that had happened? How stupid could I be? But I couldn't let my embarrassment sidetrack me. "Please, Mister, I need you to radio the Ghan for me."

He nodded. "What's the message?"

"You have to tell them that the men in the compartment next to ours have a bird with them."

The man raised one eyebrow. "You better hurry, kids. Your engineer just climbed up into the train. This has been a longer-than-usual stop as it is."

"Won't you call on the radio first?" said Eve. "Please."

"Best to talk that over with your engineer. Hurry now." The man made a sweeping motion with his hands. "You'll miss your train." He shook his head as if to himself and stretched out on the cot again.

"Right." I backed out of the station. No one would believe us, no one would make a radio call for us, unless we presented things a lot more carefully. "Thanks anyway."

CHAPTER 8

Billy

The engine was already roaring. "Hold it!" I shouted. "Wait up!" I ran across the platform, waving like a maniac.

Frederick looked down at me. But it wasn't Frederick — it was the man who had been talking to Frederick earlier. "Don't worry. I'm not going anywhere without you. We've got plenty of time. Frederick got here way ahead of schedule."

"What happened to Frederick?" called Eve from right behind me.

"We traded shifts. It's a long haul. Frederick could use a break." The man laughed. "It gets mighty tedious. Mighty easy to fall asleep on the job." His laugh was as easy as his words. I felt a tiny spark of hope. "Well, don't just stand there, climb on in." He extended his right hand. He was missing two fingers.

I was too surprised to act right; I stared. Then I stole a glance at his other hand; it was normal. I looked at his face in confusion. Everything was crazy. I didn't like the idea of traveling with this stranger. But if we were going to stop Beaky and No Brains, we had to get moving fast.

"Billy," he said. "At your service." His mouth was cockeyed even when he spoke — the right side was higher than the left. It was a pleasant effect — a lot better than the effect of a three-digit hand. "Come on, now." He stretched that hand even farther.

We didn't need help climbing in, but it would be rude to refuse it. I took Billy's hand, trying to make sure I held it as firmly as I would a normal hand. I didn't want him to think I thought any less of him because he had only three digits. I climbed in. Then I watched while Billy helped Eve in. "I'm Zach and this is Eve."

Billy bowed. "Welcome. Let's hit the tracks." He grinned as the train pulled out.

I couldn't believe how easy his grin was, how

easy his laugh had been. Everything about Billy seemed easy. My tiny hope now ballooned and soared. I smiled like a fool. I was suddenly euphoric. Things were going to work out. The sky was lightening up just slightly and the predawn desert air came in cool and sweet through the open window on the top half of the door. At night having that door window open would have frozen us. But now I liked it. It gave a wonderful free feeling to the ride. I took off my blanket poncho.

Eve looked at me with a question on her face. I kept on smiling. She smiled back uncertainly. Then she leaned over Billy's shoulder. "How does this thing run?"

"Thinking about becoming an engineer, is that it?" Billy laughed. "The controls take a man's strength. Or some of them do, at least. Like this brake here." He pointed to a tall lever. "Listen, it's still a good while till full morning, why don't you try to catch a wink? Settle down on those cushions."

I looked around. To the right of the door were two old cushions that had tie strings at the corners. They'd obviously been taken off someone's chairs. "Did you bring the cushions, Billy?"

"Yup. I heard I'd be carrying guests." He laughed. "You have to treat guests right, now, don't ya?"

"Thank you," I said.

Eve went over to the cushions and sat down, but I stayed standing by Billy.

Billy pulled on a big knob and the train lurched ahead a little faster now. He held his hand on the knob. Whenever we seemed to slow down, he turned it to the right and we'd go faster. But, in fact, we weren't going very fast at all. Not nearly as fast as with Frederick. "Let's speed up. We'll never get to Port Augusta at this rate."

"Oh, we'll get there," said Billy. "This is my job. I do it right." He didn't speed up.

The light on the instrument console, the one I'd noticed last night, went on again. Billy turned the little lever near the light ninety degrees. The light went off. He looked ahead at the tracks with a satisfied, half-dreamy expression.

I wanted to ask him about that light, but first things first. "Please, we're in a hurry."

"We'll get there. I do what I'm paid to do."

"But . . ."

153

"Not another word. We'll get there when we're supposed to get there."

The words were firm enough — the set of his shoulders, the tone of his voice, were even firmer. Billy wasn't about to be urged on by me. I had to mull this over. Maybe he wasn't as easy a guy as I'd figured.

Eve kept her eyes on me. I could see she thought I had a plan and she was waiting for me to tell her what to do next. I didn't have a plan. On the other hand, Eve didn't know that. I winked at her just to see what she'd do.

Eve stood up. "Boom!" she shouted. "Boom, boom, boom, boom!"

Billy jumped about a foot into the air. He swirled around. "What?"

"Boom!" shouted Eve.

"What on earth?"

"Boom!"

By this time I was doubled over laughing. "Billy's not a squirrel, Evil."

"Chipmunk," said Eve. Then she rubbed her stomach. "But probably squirrels act the same. I'm hungry."

Billy looked from Eve to me to Eve and back to me again. He gave a weak smile. "Is she okay?"

"No, she's totally crazy," I said.

"You should have warned me."

"I'm hungry," said Eve.

Billy nodded. "Sure. Right. Look in the Esky. Over there."

Shoved against the far wall hidden in the shadows were two picnic coolers — the little one Billy had been holding when I first saw him, and a larger one. Eve knelt down beside them. She knew right off that they called them Eskies. We had used a cooler with Mom's friends in Alice Springs the day we went to Simpson's Gap, but I hadn't noticed what they'd called them. Eve apparently had. Maybe she really was better at languages than I was. But she was still crazy. "Boom," I whispered to her as I knelt beside her and opened the big one. "Boom. That has got to be the dumbest thing you ever did."

"At least I did something," Eve whispered back. "You haven't tried anything yet and we're going at a snail's pace."

Billy glanced at us over his shoulder. "Not the big one. The big one's got lunch. Morning tucker is in the little one."

I shut the big cooler — the Esky — and I opened the little one.

Eve grabbed the package of iced cinnamon rolls. She ripped it open and stuffed one in her face. You'd think she hadn't eaten for days. How could she act like such a pig, I wondered as I wolfed down my second roll.

"Any left for me?" Billy laughed.

Eve got up and handed him a roll.

"Tah," he said.

"You're welcome," said Eve.

Sometimes I wanted to kill Eve. Tah. How did she know "tah" meant "thank you"? It sounded like baby talk.

I sifted through the stuff in the cooler. There were oranges, two other kinds of fruit I didn't recognize, a plastic bag with buttered bread cut in triangles, two bottles of juice, napkins, paper cups, and a bag of ice. "You thirsty, Billy?"

"I had coffee just before starting up, but I guess I could use a little something."

I put ice in two cups and poured Billy and me

some mixed mango-pineapple juice. I walked over beside Billy and handed him one of the cups.

"Tah," said Billy.

Eve took the other cup from me. "Tah." She drank happily.

I made a face at her just for fun and went back and poured myself another cup.

Billy smiled over his shoulder at us. "It's nice to have your company. I'm used to a lot of empty time out here."

I walked over and stood on one side of Billy while Eve stood on the other. "What state are you from?"

"New South Wales." Billy drank his juice.

"Do you miss home?" I asked.

"Sometimes." He nodded. "Grew up on a chicken farm."

"Bgok," clucked Eve. "Bgok, bgok, bgok, bgok."

Billy looked at Eve with caution on his face. "White leghorns, and brown ones, too. And some bantams. Especially bantam roosters."

"Cockadoodledoo," said Eve. But she said it good. She sounded pretty much like a rooster.

Billy laughed. "What's she, the sound-effects woman?"

"No. She's a bird."

"Am not," said Eve.

"Are, too."

"Well, now. She doesn't look like a bird to me," said Billy with great fervor. "She looks like a very nice young lady."

Billy seemed to be into this argument, and I wanted to keep him talking and get him to loosen up as much as possible. "She can fly," I said. Eve couldn't fly, of course, but it was all I could think of to keep him talking.

"Flying doesn't make a bird," said Eve. "What about bats?"

"And planes," said Billy.

Yikes! I wanted them to be into it, sure, but now they were ganging up on me! "She lays eggs," I said stupidly, looking Eve up and down. "She's got a beak."

Eve and Billy looked at each other. "The duck-billed platypus," they said together, dissolving in a fit of laughter.

I took Billy's cup and went to refill it.

"No more juice, mate. I've had enough for

now." Billy laughed. "Want to know about birds? See here." He pointed at Eve's hand. "She's got five fingers. Now that's not your typical bird. Take a look at this." Billy held up his right hand, the one missing two fingers. "There's a proper bird extremity. A chicken foot. Except I'm missing the rear balancing toe. I guess I was born to live on a chicken farm."

"Were you born with just a thumb and two fingers?" asked Eve.

"Nah." Billy looked at us and hesitated. Then he thrust his chin forward and spoke in a creaky voice. "A great white got me."

"A shark?" I swallowed hard. I'd read about Australia's shark attacks. "A shark bit your fingers off?"

Billy laughed. "Makes a good story, doesn't it?" He shook his head. "Nah. The real truth is a lot more ordinary. Cancer."

"That's awful," said Eve.

"At the time I wasn't so happy. But it's amazing how the body adjusts. They took off my index finger and middle finger, but see how my ring finger just moved over to the middle like that?" He spread his fingers and it was true —

his ring finger was smack in the middle. "I can even write, just about as good as I did before, too." He smiled.

The light on the instrument console went on again. "That light," I said quickly. "Frederick said it was insurance. What's it for?"

"Frederick's right: cheap insurance." Billy laughed. "Just wait."

I kept my eyes on the light. A few seconds later a buzzer went off.

Billy turned the little lever ninety degrees. The buzzer and light went off. Billy nodded at me. "Every fifteen minutes that light goes on. I have thirty seconds to turn the lever. If I don't, the buzzer goes on. Then I have sixty seconds to turn the lever. If I don't, an automatic system throws the brake."

"How come?" asked Eve.

"It's called the dead man switch. That way, if I were to have a heart attack out here all alone, the locomotive would stop and you wouldn't have a runaway train screaming along the tracks." Billy smiled. "Now if the railroad weren't so cheap, they'd have two engineers in every train. We could be mates. That would be a whole lot better."

Eve put her hand on Billy's shoulder. "It must be really lonely, out here by yourself night and day."

"Well, it's not that bad." Billy gave a little sigh. "Though sometimes I miss everyone and everything. And talking about home with you two now makes me miss it more than ever. You know what else we had when I was a boy? Goats." He looked at Eve. "Nubian goats, the kind with long, floppy ears."

"Nahahahaha," bleated Eve. "Nahahaha."

"Nahahahaha," bleated Billy back. "That's why they named me Billy. Nahahahaha."

I couldn't believe it. They were both out of their minds. "No more animal sounds!" I shouted. "Stop being jerks."

Billy looked at me, surprised. Then he pursed his lips. "What's yer problem, mate?"

I thought about that. Maybe it was time to just let it all out. I studied his face. He seemed to like us, truly like us. I was just about to speak, when Eve did.

"Oh, look!" Eve lifted her face to the sky and pointed. "Look. You can see the ozone hole. Right there. It forms a spooky ring around the moon. Like a wicked halo."

"You idiot," I said. "Ozone isn't visible to the naked eye. You can't see it."

"Maybe you can't," said Billy. "But that doesn't mean Eve can't."

For a brief moment I wondered if Billy was a lunatic. But there was no time to dwell on it. He asked what my problem was and I was going to tell him. "We need to get back on the Ghan."

"Yeah. It's a lot of money to pay to ride in a freight train." He laughed.

"Can we speed up?" I looked at Billy with every ounce of earnestness in me smeared across my face. "Please."

"Feathers," said Eve.

Billy looked at her. Then the right side of his mouth rose up in that cockeyed smile. "You're right. Only birds have feathers. Do you have feathers, Eve?"

"Nope."

"Well, that settles it then," said Billy, turning to me. "She's no bird."

I sighed. "Please, both of you. Focus on the problem. We've got to catch up with the Ghan at Port Augusta. Frederick promised me we'd do that."

Billy sighed, too. He looked ahead at the tracks. "I'm supposed to bring this train into Port Augusta on schedule — not late, not early — on schedule. That's what I'm paid to do."

"Why's everyone talking about Port Augusta?" said Eve. "I thought we were going to Adelaide."

"Port Augusta's the Ghan's only stop between here and Adelaide," said Billy. "But the Ghan is scheduled to leave a good half hour before we arrive. So we're not going to catch it."

"Oh. I get it." Eve spoke softly and a little sadly. "If you went faster, you could catch it. Only you'd arrive earlier than scheduled. Oh." Then she seemed to perk up. "But that would be okay, wouldn't it? I mean, no one will care if you're early. Why should they? It's only being late that's bad."

I stood beside Billy and smiled encouragingly. Evil's logic was impeccable — even I could see that.

Billy kept his eyes on the tracks as he talked.

"What's all the fuss? This freight train's a lot more exciting than the Ghan. Here, I'll let you drive it for a while, okay? You'll have something to tell your friends about when you get home. A real Australian experience."

"It's not being on the Ghan that matters," I said. "It's catching up with some men."

"Two bad men," said Eve.

"What bad men?"

And so we told him. The whole story. Billy never said a doubting word. He just listened. Once he asked me to describe Beaky and No Brains to him in detail. But other than that, he didn't interrupt. It was a long story. He had to turn the lever for the dead man's switch twice during it.

"Do you know what you're telling me?" Billy finally looked at us. "You've met up with bird smugglers."

"What do you mean?"

"They catch the great birds, our national heritage, up there, in the Northern Territory where you came from. Then they smuggle them out of the country and sell them to rich people in other countries. It's big business." Billy turned the accelerator knob to the right as he spoke. "Big, big business."

"They thought they had a palm cockatoo — an endangered bird," said Eve. "And the black cockatoo is protected — so it's almost endangered, too. That makes it worse than normal smuggling. They didn't even care about which birds are becoming extinct."

"Of course not. All they care about is their money. There's a lot of money in bird smuggling." Billy turned the knob way to the right. "A palm cockatoo! One of our most beautiful birds, too. And I've always loved black cockatoos, as well." The train barreled along now.

I squeezed his arm. "So you're going to help us? Tah."

Eve looked at me, surprised. Then she smiled in pure happiness. I never should have used an Australian word. Now I'd have to put up with her satisfaction. She kissed Billy's cheek. "I knew you would. I just knew you would. And you won't get in trouble for arriving early. No one could blame you."

"We'll make it, love." Billy nodded his head emphatically. "I'm usually known for getting in ahead of schedule." He laughed. "That's the ironic part. People are always on my case for speeding. But this time I was going by the schedule." He shook his head. "The Ghan should arrive at Port Augusta by twelve-fifteen if she's on her regular schedule. We'll be there right behind her, we will."

"Oh, look. The sun's coming up." Eve pointed. "The sun's coming up and the moon's staying anyway."

"Let's drink to that," I said. I refilled all our cups with mango-pineapple juice. "To the sun and the moon," I said, lifting my cup.

"Kree," said Eve. She lifted her cup.

"Kree," answered Billy in a pretty good cockatoo imitation. "Kree, kree, kree." He raised his cup to meet Eve's. "Around a farm, just about everyone's a sound-effects man. I was pretty good at it when I was little, too. Just like you. Kree!"

Eve burst out in a magpie's song and Billy joined her. I never thought I'd be grateful for my sister's birdcalls, but I was then. She was clearly the reason we'd become friends with Billy.

"Do you like Willie Wagtail?" Eve wagged her butt and sang.

Billy gave huge belly laughs. "That's a great giggle all right." Then he sobered up. "Willie's always been special to me, you know, because we share the same name. We're both short for William." Billy nodded as though what he'd just said was of huge import. "You know what the Aborigines say about old Willie?"

"No," said Eve. "I know what they say about Kookaburra. You can't imitate Kookaburra."

"That's right. The old laughing Jack."

"Who's laughing Jack?"

"Why, that's Kookaburra's other name. And then they call him Jackass, too." Billy clapped his hands together and dropped them in his lap. "Do you think he sounds like a Jackass?"

"No," said Eve. "Tell me about Willie Wagtail."

The light in the console went on. I reached up and turned the lever ninety degrees.

Billy smiled at me. Then he winked at Eve. "Well, you can't tell secrets in front of Willie because he'll tell everyone else. So you just never talk in front of him."

"Never?" said Eve.

"Never never never," said Billy, and he

laughed at nothing. "But I can keep a secret." He bobbed his head up and down emphatically and turned the acceleration knob even more to the right.

"What the hell is going on?" came a voice behind me.

I jumped around, my heart in my throat.

Eve grabbed my arm.

No Brains stood in front of an open bathroom door. I didn't even know the locomotive had a bathroom. "What do you think you're doing? This is going way too fast! Slow her down."

I was too stunned to do anything. I just looked from No Brains to Billy.

Billy turned the knob to the right. I watched the rpm's move up. The arrow had to be close to the danger point that Frederick had shown me. Maybe it was already.

"I said, slow this thing down!" No Brains pushed me aside and shouted in Billy's ear. "Slow it down!"

Billy looked straight ahead. "I won't let you steal birds from my country. I don't know what kind of Australian you are, but you're not getting any help from me."

"What are you talking about? These kids are crazy. They make up a dizzy story and you believe them?"

"That's right."

"The kids don't know anything."

"The girl knows birds. You don't have a palm cockatoo, that's for sure."

No Brains threw back his head. "It better be a palm cockatoo."

"It isn't," said Eve, piping up from behind me. She seemed to know just where to stand when she wanted to be courageous.

"Slow down this train!"

"No!" Billy shook his head. "And to think I was going to bring this train in on schedule for a mere fifty dollars. I didn't even ask what was up." He slapped his thigh. "Here I go and tell Frederick I need to take his shift for him, and it all seems like just an easy bit of money. What a dummy you took me for."

"You're crazy," said No Brains.

Billy lifted his chin to No Brains. "I'm not crazy, I'm angry. I'm going to radio ahead to the Ghan and they'll have the authorities waiting to nab you." He reached for the radio.

"No you're not!" No Brains grabbed the radio and ripped the cord out. He dropped it on the floor.

Eve picked up the radio and cradled it like a sick baby. "Oh no," she said, backing away toward the side. "Oh no."

Billy stood up. He wobbled a bit, the train was going so fast. Then he swung his fist at No Brains. No Brains grabbed him around the chest. I jumped on No Brains from behind. No Brains staggered backwards. He reached one hand around and ripped me off his back. Then he hit me across the chest with the back of his arm. It was a bear swipe. I flew up and backwards. I slammed against the door. The latch gave way and the door swung out over nothing, taking me with it.

CHAPTER 9

Out of Control

Eve screamed.

My arms flew up and I managed to twist and grab hold of the window opening in the door as I fell. My face slammed against the metal. I heard a little pop inside my head, as though my nose had broken. I was flat against the door, but I wasn't really hanging there. We were going so fast, the wind pinned me in place at first, then pushed at me. The lower part of my body was swept backwards, and now I was hanging on to the door with my full strength. All I could think of was those huge, loud wheels below. I had to keep myself from falling under them. I hung on desperately, half wild. The door was too thick to offer my hands an easy hold. It was hard, so hard. My feet were now out to the side, beyond the edge of the door. They hit something rigid and vertical. And I realized it was the ladder that went up the outside to the roof. I braced both feet against the side of the ladder and stayed that way, slanted and mashed against the door. I clenched my fingers around the thick top window edge of the door as best I could manage and tighter than I'd ever held on to anything or anyone in my life.

My chest hurt from No Brains's blow, and my nose and right cheek ached from slamming into the door, and my hands were already sore, and I felt completely out of breath as though I were dying. But I wasn't. I was breathing. I was clinging to this door, braced against the ladder, alive. The wind stung my eyes. The engine roared around me. And I held on.

Eve was screaming and screaming.

The men were shouting. I knew they were still fighting. I knew it was a horrible, brutal fight.

Eve's head poked out the open door and she looked back, tears streaming down her face. Her jaw dropped when she saw me. She held out her arm. I knew I could touch her hand if I let go with my left hand, and I knew her hand would be a lot easier to hold on to than this door. But I didn't like her leaning that far through the opening. "Get the wrench," I shouted. "The wrench."

Eve disappeared. I prayed Billy would keep No Brains busy long enough for Eve to grab the wrench and for me to get back inside. It would take little effort for No Brains to throw Eve off the train — just one vicious toss. My little sister.

Eve appeared again. She extended the wrench with both her hands so tight on it, they shone white at the knuckles.

All I had to do was hold on to the wrench with one hand and keep hold of the window edge of the door with the other. And if I kept one foot braced against the ladder with most of my weight on it until the very last moment, Eve would never be pulling too much weight. I had to make sure she didn't pull too much weight. I had to make sure she didn't fall out of the train. "If you feel me falling, Eve, let go," I shouted.

"Just grab it, Zach!" she shouted back.

Her little face was all squinched up. I knew she wouldn't let go, no matter what happened. Just like I'd never let go of her if we'd been reversed. The wind took my breath away. I looked down. At this speed, we'd die if we fell. Billy had turned the accelerator knob way to the right — we were going at a dangerous speed. How long had it been since the last time the dead man's switch light had gone on? I needed that automatic brake. I needed the train to stop. I had turned the lever myself, right before No Brains came out of the bathroom. It seemed like years ago, but it couldn't have been more than ten minutes. That meant five more minutes before the train would even start to brake. And now I remembered Frederick's words — with this copper load and at this increasing speed, it would take extra long to brake.

I couldn't just stay hanging on to the door. It took so much strength to hang there, I'd never be able to do it till the train finally stopped. My hands felt like they'd give any minute. I had to risk it.

I let go of the door and grabbed hold of the wrench with my left hand.

Eve pressed herself up against the wall on the near side of the door and held the wrench firm.

"Come on, Zach," she called. "You can do it."
She pulled the wrench toward her a little.

I was stretched about as far as I could go without giving up my footholds. There was no little sill outside the door. There was nothing extra to help me. This was it. I either made it, or we both died. I lunged with my left foot and left arm simultaneously. Eve pulled the wrench toward her. My left foot reached the door hole, and now my right foot hung free. I was spread eagle, pressed against the train, one hand on the wrench, the other on the door, one foot in the train, the other dangling. I tried to hop my right hand along the window edge of the door closer to the opening, but it was too hard — the door edge was too thick. I had to let go of the door and grab the wrench with both hands. Could Eve take my weight like that? My heart beat violently. I pushed off with my right hand and grabbed the wrench. Eve pulled simultaneously with all her strength. I lurched into the locomotive, plowing into Eve. We both crashed to the floor, the wrench painfully pressed between us.

I scrambled to my feet, pulling Eve up with

me. But I didn't think fast enough. The wrench, that wonderful wrench, slipped off her and got kicked out the door in the shuffle. It was our only serious weapon of defense, and now it was gone.

No Brains had his back to us. He knelt on the floor by Billy and slapped his face. "You idiot. You stupid idiot. You have to drive this train."

But No Brains was the idiot for hitting Billy so hard. Billy was sprawled on the floor, out cold; anyone could see that. Slapping wasn't going to bring him to.

The locomotive was rocking now, we were going so fast. A fold-out table fell off the wall, its screws jiggled free from the motion.

"We're going to jump the track," shouted Eve.

No Brains stood up. He stared at me. "I thought I got rid of you. What's the matter with you kids, that no one can get rid of you?" He lifted his arm to strike.

"I can drive the train," I said quickly. "And you can't."

No Brains looked confused at that. He stood with his arm in the air. I wanted to make some mental joke about how stupid he was, but I couldn't think of any. He dropped his arm. "What do you know about driving a train?"

"Billy taught me everything," I lied.

No Brains grabbed Eve by the arm. "All right. You get this train under control right now, or your sister goes over the side."

I ran to the controls and turned the knob to the left.

Buzz! A red light on the panel board flashed and buzzed simultaneously.

"What's that mean?" said No Brains.

"How should I know?" Panic tightened my chest. Why didn't the dead man's switch go off? "You're the one who pulled out the radio. Now we can't even call for instructions." I turned the knob more to the left. If we were slowing down, I couldn't tell it yet. I looked at the rpm's. They were way over the danger point.

Buzz, buzz. Flash, flash.

"Look!" shouted Eve.

I looked. Sure enough, another train was ahead on the tracks, just barely visible now. And there were things moving on both sides of the tracks. Animals. But not camels. They were shorter than camels.

I pulled on the brake lever. The train whistle went off. We were slowing down fast. But we were also coming up on the other train fast.

"It's the Ghan!" shouted Eve.

"It's stopped!" I shouted back. "Help me. Help me pull on the brake or we're going to crash into her."

No Brains came alive at last. He took over the brake lever from me and pressed with both arms and his chest.

The light on the console went off. After an eternity, the dead man's buzzer went off.

I knew the automatic brake should be kicking in now. But even with No Brains and me and the automatic brake, we didn't seem to be stopping any faster. The wheels screeched, but we were still gaining fast on the Ghan.

"Bloody wild cattle!" shouted No Brains. "The Ghan stopped because of the bloody wild cattle!"

"We're going to crash!" screamed Eve.

The noise of the wheels and brakes was deafening. We were definitely starting to slow down, but we were also definitely closing in on the Ghan. I could now see that the animals spread out on both sides of the Ghan were cattle. They were everywhere. A big bull walked onto the tracks behind the Ghan and looked right at us. He had wide horns and a dark brown dusty coat and the stupidest face I'd ever seen. He was totally unaware he was about to become hamburger.

No Brains let go of the brake and ran for the open door. He jumped out.

I threw myself on the brake with all my weight. "Jump out, Eve!" I yelled. "Jump and roll! Before we hit them. Go on! I've got to stay holding the brake. You go!"

"Not again," screamed Eve. She pressed on me, adding her weight to the brake. "I'd rather crash than jump again."

I wanted to tell her she'd be okay. She'd been okay last time. She'd be okay this time. But I didn't get the chance.

The brakes squealed horrendously. The whole locomotive shook violently. I braced for the crash. Instead, we stopped with a jolt and a weird scream filled the air. It was the bull. His tail was caught between a railing on the back of the Ghan and the cowcatcher on the front of our freight train. He struggled like a maniac.

"The bull's alive," said Eve, half in a daze, supporting herself against the instrument panel. "He got hit by a train and he lived."

"We're alive, too," I said, pulling her to the door. "Let's run."

Eve chewed at her bottom lip as she looked around at the cattle on all sides. "Will they trample us?"

After what we'd been through, it would be anticlimactic to get trampled by cattle. I almost laughed at the thought. "I doubt they'll even notice us. After all, they hardly noticed a speeding freight train." I spoke confidently, but I was bluffing. The cattle were big. Still, all cattle were dumb, weren't they? And this was our chance. "Come on. Stay with me. We can catch Beaky now."

Eve didn't need any other encouragement. We climbed down and ran a twisted path through meandering cattle to the rear of the Ghan. The closest door was shut. I banged on it, but my fist didn't make enough noise for anyone to hear.

We ran alongside the train till we saw a woman looking out at the cattle. I picked up a rock and threw it up at the window. The woman looked at me with alarm on her face. I was pretty sure she was the same woman I'd seen in her slip when I opened her compartment door the day before. She jumped back from the window. A few seconds later, her face reappeared with a man's. She pointed at me and jabbered something. I yelled, but the window was closed and they didn't know what I was saying. Eve stepped in front of me and put her hands together as if she was praying, and looked pathetic. The man and woman disappeared.

Within minutes the doors at the end of every train carriage opened simultaneously. A porter leaned out of the closest door. "Is that the young Americans?"

"It's us, all right!" I ran to the porter and climbed up into the train with Eve right behind me.

"Well now, this is the Gambling Car. You can't . . ." he began.

I pushed past the porter and ran down the length of the carriage. Eve was at my heels. We went through into the next carriage. It was the Entertainment Car. That meant we had a full seven carriages to run through to get to our carriage. I ran faster. Eve panted behind me.

People called to us from both sides. Someone said something about the police. A little girl clapped as we zipped by. A man took hold of my arm. I shook him off and kept running.

We went right through the dining car. Beaky sat at a table near the end. He looked up and saw me coming. He stared, dumbfounded. I ran past and pulled the tablecloth off his table. A pot of hot tea spilled in his lap. He screamed. I threw the tablecloth over his head.

We raced into our carriage and went straight for Beaky and No Brains's compartment door. It was locked, of course. I shouted, "Eugene! Eugene!"

Eugene came running from the other end of the corridor.

"Open it."

"What?" Eugene looked flabbergasted. "What's . . ."

"Just open it," I shouted.

"Right now," shouted Eve.

Eugene tried the handle. His face showed surprise. He took out his keys and opened the door.

"*Kree!*" screamed the cockatoo.

Eve ran to the cage and opened the door.

"*Kree!*" The cockatoo hopped from the cage and flew out of the compartment.

I ran into the corridor after it. It headed toward the dining car just as Beaky entered our carriage. It flew right into Beaky's face.

"Help!" shouted Beaky. The air was full of flapping arms and wings. Feathers flew.

I didn't know what I was going to do till I did it. I took a flying leap at Beaky's ankles, tackled him, and bit him in the calf.

Eve stepped on me as she squirmed her way past us, calling out, "Kree, kree!" louder than the cockatoo.

And suddenly the flapping was over. The cockatoo had flown out the rear carriage door. I got up and ran to Eve and we watched the bird's wide black wings conquer the air. She turned and threw her arms around my neck. "We did it, Zach. He's free like he ought to be. Oh, I love you."

Before I could even pry Eve loose, Beaky burst

past us and jumped out the carriage door. He fell in the sand. Then he got up and ran after the bird. A big bull came loping along at that very moment. It had a crooked tail, as though it had been mashed. It lowed loudly and angrily. When it saw Beaky, it charged.

CHAPTER 10

The Hat

We were heroes, of course, Eve and me and even Billy. It turned out the police were waiting in Port Augusta to arrest the birdnappers, after all. Frederick had radioed them. The detail about the stocking had worried him and finally convinced him; it seemed like something children wouldn't imagine. That's why he'd sped up the train and managed to get us to Tarcoola so early. Anyway, no one among the train personnel on the Ghan had done anything because they were all waiting for the police. No one wanted to tangle with dangerous characters if it wasn't necessary. (And no one at that point knew that it was just one dangerous character, Beaky, since no one had seen No Brains get off the Ghan at Tarcoola.)

All that meant that even if Eve and Billy and I hadn't caught up with the Ghan, the birdnappers would have been captured. Still, the papers called us heroes because it was us who actually caught them, and we didn't argue with the papers. When we got back to America, our local paper ran a story on us, too.

Geoffrey Froder and Paul Lima, as Beaky and No Brains were named in ordinary life, turned state's witness and blabbed on a ring of thieves that stole natural treasures from Australia and smuggled them out of the country. The ring had started with fossils and then moved on to rare animals. They sold them to eccentric wealthy people all over the world, just as Billy had said. Apparently, getting people to catch the animals was no problem for the thieves. The big problem was getting the animals out of the country. Alice Springs had no international airport. So they had to take the birds from the outback and travel to a city with a big airport. They chose Adelaide to smuggle out of because Adelaide's international airport was the most lax on customs of all the airports in Australia. All Adelaide usually checked for was metal. And the smugglers took the Ghan to Adelaide rather than an airplane because the Ghan had no baggage check.

So long as Beaky could convince the train crew that the birdcage was a prop for his clown act, any smuggled birds could travel in the passenger cars with them. And, in fact, posing as a clown meant people who just happened to see a protected bird in the cage couldn't realize the significance of what they'd seen. I mean, if an ordinary person has a rare bird in a cage, you think he's a criminal. But if a clown does, you hardly give it any thought.

Now the government was going after the big smuggling ring and Beaky and No Brains would get off light. Or relatively light. Beaky had a sore bottom from his encounter with the bull. I read in the papers that he couldn't sit down for a week. It was satisfying to imagine that huge butt all tender and swollen. And No Brains had sprained an ankle when he jumped from the train. That made sense. After all, it takes brains to know to roll.

And both of them were still in trouble for

throwing us off the train — they'd get jail time for that. Plus, No Brains was in trouble for his extra part in things. When Beaky and No Brains heard Eugene's announcement that we'd been picked up by a freight train and that we'd catch up with the Ghan at Port Augusta, they knew they had to slow down the freight train somehow. So No Brains snuck off the Ghan when it stopped at Tarcoola and bribed Billy. From Billy's point of view it was all innocent. He admitted he'd taken the fifty dollars, but he took it as passage to get No Brains to Port Augusta at the exact scheduled time of arrival for the freight train. So he thought he was taking money just to do his job. He didn't know No Brains was trying to keep us from the Ghan. And Frederick hadn't urged Billy to get to Port Augusta early because he knew of Billy's reputation for speeding, and he just took it for granted that Billy would easily get there early, given that the freight train was already ahead of schedule when it arrived at Tarcoola.

We backed up Billy's story, of course, and vouched for him all the way. So No Brains stood accused of trainnapping. But none of it was much compared to the long jail sentences the other thieves in the smuggling ring would get.

If we hadn't stopped them, Beaky and No Brains would have been paid thousands for that one red-tailed black cockatoo. A real palm cockatoo would have sold for up to $30,000. And the eventual owner of the bird would have paid the head of the smuggling ring much, much more. But that's all supposing that the bird had lived. We learned that most of these birds die in captivity. And almost none of them reproduce in captivity. So all that smuggling results in a lot of death and waste.

Eve liked to repeat those facts. Just last night she told them to Mom for the zillionth time. Mom said, "I'm so proud of you," just as she had done for a zillion other times over the past month. Then she added, "You're brave."

"Me?" said Eve, twirling around the leather cap on her head — Dad's cap — the one I gave her the night we got back. I just took out the box of Dad's old things and handed it to her fast, before I could stop myself. She held it in her hands and stared without a word, till I took it from her and put it on her head. She slept with it that night and she's worn it all day every day since. "Do you know how scared I would have been if I'd gone through any of that by myself? I can barely even stand to think about being thrown off the Ghan like we were. If I'd been alone, I'd have been so scared, I'd probably have died." Eve looked at me. "But Zach wasn't afraid. Never. Not even when he hung on the door out the side of the train. He's a great survivor. He's like the cockatoo that got away." She smiled and lifted her cap in salute.

And I smiled back.

Donna Jo Napoli is the acclaimed author of several books for middle-grade children, including *When the Water Closes over My Head*, named a "Children's Book of the Year" by the Bank Street/Child Study Children's Book Commitee, and *The Prince of the Pond*, selected for the New York Public Library's *100 Titles — For Reading and Sharing*. Her novels for older children include *The Magic Circle* and, for Scholastic Press, *Song of the Magdalene*. Ms. Napoli is Chair of the Department of Linguistics at Swarthmore College. A visit to Australia to teach writing for children at the University of Queensland included the twenty-two-hour train trip across the outback which inspired this story. Ms. Napoli lives in Swarthmore, Pennsylvania, with her family.